Shad‹

By Crystal Spears

ISBN-13: 978-1502570710

Author Crystal Spears

Author.CrystalD.Spears@gmail.com

Author

Crystal Spears

Editor

Katie Mac @ Indie Express LLC
(https://www.facebook.com/Indieexpress)

Graphic Design

Melissa Gill @ MGBookCovers
(https://www.facebook.com/MGbookcovers)

Formatting

Crystal Spears (https://www.facebook.com/CrystalDawnSpears)

A letter from the author,

Dear Readers,

If you haven't read Seize Me, Withstanding Me, or Resenting Me, this novel will make no sense to you. Since it is a continuing series, I don't flashback a whole lot to describe characters to you. It would take at least two chapters to do so and there are way too many characters in the Breakneck series to do that. I have a request to make. Please do not reveal the major plot points such as deaths or births in your reviews. I'd really appreciate it. Before you go on to read Shadowing Me, please understand, due to Shadow's extensive background outside of Breakneck, this is the reasoning behind the way I wrote this novel and the reason for Shadow's crossover into my upcoming novel Pain of Mine. Remember, remember, and remember that tiny detail. You will also find that Shadowing Me is a tad different than the first three Breakneck releases. There is a reason for that as well. Take a moment and count the characters I have in this series. The number is up there. All my characters are very different from one another and some come from a completely different background than Breakneck. In the past few Breakneck releases, I tried to give you a little of the main characters POVs. I hardly did that in Shadowing Me. This gives me more room to have the characters grow and lets me focus more solely on them. I will be re-releasing Seize Me and Withstanding Me in the near future. There will a few changes.

Tatiana's hair color is now blonde. In Seize Me it was brown. The name of the BDSM club and the name of Shadow's friend changed as well. These changes were necessary.

With all that said, I would like to thank all of my readers and followers for wishing me well over this past year. It's been a rough year and I am thankful that my health is better and I am back to work writing full time.

You were the reasons I opened my laptop back up and pushed through it. So thank you from the bottom of my heart.

Crystal Spears

Dedication

To those who have felt defeated a time or two in their lifetime.

We only live once, so make it count.

When you're down, look up to the sky, smile, and pick yourself back up again.

Chapter One

Shadow

I slam hard into the nameless mouth, willing and begging her to gag on my cock. I want to inflict some kind of pain. It's true, I'm a Sadist. I have to cause a little hurt in order to cum. A fucked-up, tragic past has nothing to do with my being this way. I just require that something more to release.

Vanilla fucking doesn't do it for me. When I was fifteen, I wrapped my arm around my girlfriend's neck and strangled her as we both came. She was in shock, yet she didn't run away. She simply dressed, went over to her piece of shit computer, and waited for the slow-ass, dial-up internet to connect. She then Googled all kinds of words before anything made any sense.

My best friend gently let me down when she told me she could no longer see me. It broke my heart. We had been fucking one another since the age of thirteen, and when I cut off her air supply, it scared the living shit out of her. Who could blame her? I sure the fuck couldn't. Once I figured out exactly what I needed to get off, I sought out older women with experience. Since then, I've hurt countless women I've fucked, and they've enjoyed it.

See, this bitch with my cock in her mouth isn't doing it for me. I push away from her and curse her for being in a place like this with zero knowledge about what to expect in a room like the one where we are. This is my private room. It has a closet, a bed, a bathroom, and a dresser, and it houses all the toys I use for my particular trade.

As I zip my pants, she whines that she doesn't understand, and I pat her gently on the shoulder and tell her to do some research. She is proof that Alec is not screening new members correctly. I should have known when I spent more time explaining and giving instructions than actually screwing her.

I tap my foot, waiting for her to leave my room before I lock up and walk down the long corridor that houses the private rooms. I'm not in the mood to try again, so I say goodbye to my friend, the dipshit who owns this club. He has no clue that my President and his wife are about to take it over.

I walk out and the brisk air hits my face. I pause to take a deep breath and welcome the freshness into my lungs. I was suffocating in there. There isn't anything worse than being tortured by your own fucking downfall.

I straddle my lady, start her up, and head to the clubhouse, praying I don't run into Tatiana. I want that girl bad, so fucking bad, but not even she can get my dick hard unless I think about tying her up and putting some welts on her. I have never once thought my addiction was a problem until meeting Tatiana.

When the prospect opens the gate to the clubhouse grounds, I throttle my bike in and park.

I spot Sniper and Smokey walking towards the old clubhouse building, and Sniper pats his wrist like he's wearing a watch. I nod my head in acknowledgement. I'd never miss a church meeting. He knows this, but I think the fucker needs to get laid. Pussy footing around with Piper isn't doing his dick any favors if he ain't tapping that shit. I don't think I'll ever understand what goes on between them. They claim to be very good friends, but they both hold the look that spells a four-letter word I never want to hear again. I haven't heard it since I was a teen. That fucking word can suck it.

I light a smoke as I head into church. The feel of eyes on my body causes me to stop dead in my tracks and look around. Nothing seems out of the ordinary, but the eerie sensation still doesn't ease up. Maybe I'm overly tired and aggravated that my sex life is shit. Whatever it is, it better damn well go away. I make it my business to study those around me, not the other way around. My skills are one of the main reasons the Prez let me trade up Charters instead of going nomad. If I become the one being watched, I'm not doing my damn job right. This shit is frustrating as hell.

"Damn, brother. Your eyebrows are sittin' on top of your head," Smokey says while Sniper walks in ahead of us.

"Shut the fuck, we got church. And when the fuck did you start talkin'," I question him.

"Why does everyone keep askin' me that," Smokey replies.

It's true. Smokey isn't one for words. Lately, though, he has been talking a lot, and no one can find a reason as to why he's opening up. Don't get me wrong. I enjoy that the motherfucker actually has a personality and all, but it is weird.

He shakes out his thoughts, opens the door, and gestures for me to go first.

"To answer your question, something Pyro said got me thinkin'. He said life is way too short and he may have implied that I should maybe voice my opinions or some shit. So I'm trying and it's bullshit that everyone keeps questioning me on it," Smokey growls.

Well, shit. I should have kept my mouth shut.

"I'm sorry, brother," I say as we enter the chapel and take our seats.

Smokey shrugs as he flops backwards in his leather chair. "Oh well, I'm talkin' now. Might as well keep up the charade."

I bark out a laugh. The motherfucker is sort of funny. Who would have thought? I reach across the table and stub out my smoke that I basically let burn between my fingers. So wasteful. I should just fucking quit, but that shit ain't going to happen. I guess that makes me weak, but I really don't give a shit. Chain smoking is the only thing that keeps me from wigging out on fucking idiots.

The Prez comes in, slams the door behind him, and stalks to his chair. As he sits down, he grabs the gavel and bangs it down onto the wooden plank, signaling for all attention to be directed at him.

"Breakneck brothers, it's that time again. Time for us to discuss massive fuckin' migraine topics," he huffs and digs out his pad of paper and a pen.

"Shadow, I need you to escort Winter to the doctor tomorrow. I have to run some shit by Petra, and then I'll meet ya there and you can go."

I nod, accepting my orders.

"Max, numbers," Prez asks as he starts to scribble down onto his notepad.

Max goes over treasury because he's our figures guy. He reports on the dues paid and lets us know what our cuts are for the work we've done. He also goes over the clubhouse joint account, which we call the stack pot. Our fees go into this account to cover the club bills. Each person contributes this way.

"Zig Zag, charity runs, we got any comin' up?"

"Naw, Prez, I've shifted the next two over to the lady charter. With Winter pregnant, I didn't think you'd want to run," ZZ says.

"Good, good. Let them bitches do it."

He doesn't mean that in a disrespectful way, and if anyone messes with the lady charter, it's the equivalent of messing with us.

"All right, Angel wants to take over the Chinese nail salons. She ain't changing her damn mind for nothing. I told her they pretty much run the gambling trade in Las Vegas, but she ain't up for it. She says, since they make home base here, they gotta pay up. So, any ideas for how we can keep blood outta this situation?"

Not a single one of us will fight Winter on takeovers. Bad shit has happened to her, so she likes to control the situations all around us, and that includes controlling all of Jamaica, Nevada.

"Money?" Max asks if we can offer up money in exchange for them to leave first. You always offer first, bloodshed is and always will be a last resort.

An idea comes to mind. "Well, there aren't many of them here. Hell, it's mostly their wives and a bunch of kids. So maybe offer up some startup cash for new salon locations in Las Vegas. I mean, shit, even tell them the truth. Your wife is dead set on owning a couple of salons, and you're tryin' to keep the peace and all that jazz."

"That could actually work," he says while he writes some shit down. Prez likes to handle his own notes. The charter I was at before this, the Prez didn't do jack but talk.

"Get me some numbers to work with out of the gold pipeline money, Max. I want this transaction to be under the table if it goes well. No traces back to us."

No one questions the statement. My guess is he's not trying to use Winter's money at all for this. She's loaded and he can't stand it. He's old fashioned like the rest of us. We take care of our women, not the other way around. And the fact that Winter could take care of this entire club and all the members and their family burns him deep. I think he's still afraid if he fucks up, she has the money to leave his ass without a trail in sight, and she will disappear.

"Moving on to the BDSM club business. Shadow, you still don't think he'll sell?"

I rub my jaw. "Naw, Prez. If I'm bein' honest with ya, I think it might not be easy."

I feel like such an ass. I hate doing this to Alec, but he has screwed up time and time again by not screening the members more closely. He's not teaching the newbies the rules and bring them up to club standards.

My blood runs hot as I think back on the time Tatiana met up with this dickhead who practiced breath play on her. ZZ was ten times hotter seeing his daughter lying on the cement of the clubhouse parking lot.

"Well, we're Breakneck. We'll get it handled. We can't have that shit up in our town if it ain't bein' run properly."

I can't help but agree. BDSM, in any form, light or dark, is dangerous if the participants aren't well versed in the practice of their choosing.

"You think you could schedule a meeting with your friend?" he asks as he looks back up from his notes.

"Yeah, when?"

He pauses to think about it for a moment.

"A few weeks from now, because I want to get this shit handled with the Chinese. I want the less stressful shit first."

"Yep, I'll make a meetin' after all that's settled."

He reaches for the gavel and slams it down. It means he's satisfied and we're free to go.

***

Chapter Two

Tatiana

I smack at Storm's hand as she tries to change my answers on my homework again. Ever since we started doing our business management schooling together, she has always tried to fix my work. When she huffs at me, I smile. I have never cared about the women in my dad's life until now. He never really had a steady girlfriend until Storm, so I rarely ever paid attention to them. But Storm is different. She snagged a hold of my dad and is not letting go. He doesn't want her to either. She is good to me and my twin brother, Mason, who we didn't even know existed until a little over three months ago.

At first, I was hesitant about their relationship. I am his little girl after all, but when Storm lost my dad's baby in a car accident, it entirely changed the way I felt.

When my brother came traipsing into Club Sated, Storm could've been angry about my dad having another child after she had lost her unborn baby, but she wasn't. And that is the moment I fell in love with her. She is barely a few years older than me, and maybe it is what makes it so much easier to get along with her. I do not know. Either way, I am more than accepting when it comes to her relationship with my dad.

Like right now as we sit at the bar of Club Sated doing our homework for one of our classes, she is acting like a mother would be when it comes to homework. What is not to love about that?

The sound of glass shattering echoes all around the club.

"Dammit! This damn pregnant stomach of mine is getting all

up in my way!" Winter cries.

You can't even tell she is with child. She is only four months along. Hell, you can't even call it a stomach. It is like a small kangaroo pouch.

"You're barely showing, Win. Shut up." Piper snickers.

"Barely showing my ass. I've already gone up two pant sizes. My ass has its own zip code!"

Own zip code. I snort. She is still so tiny. After a few moments, I look over at Storm and frown. She is dazed, staring at nothing. I know she is thinking about the child she lost and it breaks my heart.

I reach over and place my hand on hers. I don't say anything because words aren't needed. Nothing I can say will ever make this okay. She handled it well when it happened, but I think as Winter's pregnancy furthers, Storm's pain is surfacing. She talks a big game, but I know she is hurting and hell, my dad still hurts, too.

Storm nods her head for me to get back to work, letting me know she is okay and that is when he enters.

I sense Shadow even before my eyes land on him. The club isn't open yet so I don't know why he is here, but he is, and now I want to get up and leave.

Shadow has a way of making me feel like I am still a child and I don't matter. And yet, I still find myself incredibly attracted to him. It plays hell on my emotions. How can you want to be with someone who makes you feel like that?

"Oh, hey, Shadow. Give me a minute and I'll be ready to go." Winter tells him.

"Where're ya going, Win," Piper asks as she stocks some more beer bottles.

Yes, I would love to know.

"Shadow has the ungodly task of taking me to the OBGYN."

I giggle. Shadow in an OBGYN office. That shit is hilarious.

"I'm not staying there," he murmurs, irritated.

"What? You don't want to see them squirt cold shit on my stomach?"

All right, so maybe not running away was the smart thing to do. It is super fun to watch an uncomfortable Shadow squirm.

"No, ma'am."

Ah, hell.

"Shadow!" Winter whines.

He said it on purpose to irritate her. Everyone knows all the women hate being called ma'am. The only one that allows it is Grandma Berry and that is only because she is getting older.

As Winter scrambles around to gather her things to leave, I take the opportunity to look at Shadow. I don't get many chances to do this. He is the watcher, not the watched.

He looks as good as he always does. Tall, dark, and handsome, all wrapped in a leather cut. Shadow's dark black hair spiked at the tips, his cologne smelling fresh, his black club bracelets tugging tightly against his wrists. His light blue jeans hang off his body enough that you can still see his thigh muscles through them. His lips stretch in a dark scowl and yet it still looks incredibly sexy on him. His whole demeanor screams 'fuck me hard', and hell if I don't want to jump on him and do that.

15

I know the kind of lifestyle Shadow is in. I've been practicing, studying, and adopting it as my own for the past several months. I may not know the very extent of his particular trade, but I do know a little about it. Pain. He loves to inflict pain. He needs to cause harm to another in order for him to cum.

One night, I followed him to a BDSM club. Shadow wouldn't touch me at all, and I figured out why. He is afraid he might scare me off.

So I made the choice to walk into the club unprepared and not knowing zip. The first few times I practiced, it was fantastic. I tried the light restraints and being gagged. It wasn't until Shadow told me he's a Sadist and loved to inflict actual pain that I dug a little deeper. That is when I messed up. I messed up horribly.

I met a guy outside the club. Instead of going inside, we decided to go to his place. Taking my practice and learning outside of the club playspace was my first mistake. My second was leaving with a man I didn't know and practicing bondage and autoerotic asphyxia with him. He beat me as I was bound, and not lightly, I might add. He caused extreme bruising to my face, and he choked me so hard that I was unconscious for too long. The man was obviously a very sick Sadist, or he had no knowledge of what the hell he was doing. I may be new at this, but even Shadow made it clear that erotic asphyxiation was not to be practiced like that. A little too late did I find out about edgeplay. It was by far the worst thing I have ever felt and done. I still study and practice the lifestyle. So far, I am leaning more towards sadomasochism, and a little bondage interests me.

At first, I did this so I could be with Shadow. After all, this is his way of life. This is what he needs, but as time has gone by, I've decided to see it through, with or without him. It interests me, and I find myself craving more. But since the club won't allow me to go back there right now, I read and try to understand everything that I can while Shadow sits in denial.

My eyes drift closed as he moves behind me. God, why does he do this to me? He leans over and deliberately places his lips to my ear. The fucker knows what he does to me. He likes to play this sick game and rile up my emotions.

"Whatcha doin', darlin'," he asks.

"What does it look like I'm doing, Shadow?"

I'll play head games right back. I'll act like I couldn't give a crap about him whispering behind me. Bastard ass!

"Tea, what's with the hostility?"

Seriously?

"Not hostile, just busy." I hit the save as button on my laptop so I don't lose all my homework. There is absolutely no way I will be able to focus with him around me. Hell, I will be lucky if I can even function when he leaves, which I hope is very soon.

"You've been a little distant, Tea. What's that about?"

Oh. My. God.

Mind games. This is what he does. Pushes and pulls, pushes and pulls, over and over again. It makes me want to turn the tables on his ass and cause bodily freaking harm!

Must. Remain. Calm, Tatiana!

"You kept pushing me away, Shadow. I'm only giving you what you wanted."

After I close my laptop and shove my papers back into a folder, I turn to face him. He looks pensive, but almost smirky at the same time. Although he looks hot in his shades, I always want

17

to rip them from his face so I can see his eyes. If I want to get answers from Shadow, I'll find them in his gaze. This is one of the main reasons he keeps them covered and masks them with blue contacts.

"Hmm…" He manages to get out minutes later.

I want to grab him by his leather cut and shake the shit out of him.

"Shadow, I'm ready to go." Winter's voice breaks our gaze from one another.

Thank god!

My shoulders slump and he takes one last look at me before turning towards Winter. Storm cackles and waits for Shadow and Winter to leave before she opens her mouth.

"Well, that wasn't tense at all…"

I smirk at her. "Very funny, Storm."

Piper puts the last bottle of whiskey away before she comes back to the bar, leans in, knots her hands under her chin, and stares at me.

No, that isn't weird at all.

"You're creeping me the hell out, Piper."

She looks at Storm before they burst out in laughter. They are trying to get a rise out of me and I am doing my best to refrain from letting my age show. I may not be much younger than they are, but that doesn't stop me from wanting to act more mature.

"You think it's too early for them to know what the baby is?"

Storm sighs before answering Piper. "Probably so, but try

telling that to Braxx."

My heart aches for her and my father, and even though Storm says she is okay with not having a baby, everyone knows it is the biggest lie of them all.

***

Chapter Three

Shadow

This is not my idea of a good time. Sitting at the doctor's office with a pregnant woman, who isn't knocked up by me, is beyond fucking uncomfortable. We aren't even here five minutes before women start staring at me. Generally, I'd take pleasure in making them squirm under my scrutiny, but they are stressing Winter out. It doesn't take a lot to figure out she is exercising a lot of patience right now. The magazine in her lap even starts to irritate her and the pages begin to crinkle under her fingertips.

"Don't you see he's fucking sitting here with a pregnant woman? I could very well be his fucking wife!"

I groan. Fuck! Where the hell is my Prez?

This has to be those pregnancy hormones he keeps bitching about.

Why in the fuck am I stuck doing this shit? Winter is a cool chick, don't get me wrong, but this is not my area of expertise. I've got to give it to her. She's handling the vultures pretty well. They really are sitting here openly staring at us, as they try to figure us out.

"Do you not see the leather he's sporting?"

A chuckle escapes my lips and her head turns towards mine, so quickly, it reminds me of the damn exorcist and I almost shiver. Hell, she can be scary. I hold my hands up in defense to remind her I am not the bad guy.

"Get my mind off these idiot women who are picturing you taking them out to the parking lot and showing them a good time."

I frown. Taking one of these women out to the parking lot is not my idea of a good time. Now, thoughts of binding her wrists behind her back and pounding ruthlessly into her dry cunt have my cock jerking inside my jeans.

"What's going on with you and Tatiana?"

Not this shit again. If I didn't know any better, I would assume everyone wants my palm print on Tea's ass, and maybe even a little blood drawn from her. Are they fucking nuts? The thought does seem more than appealing.

"Well…,"

Where the hell is my Prez? His wife is on my last nerve. I would give my right nut to get out of this conversation. That is how uncomfortable it is.

"Ain't shit going on, and to be honest with you, it's really pissing me off how everyone won't get off my goddamn case about it!"

She laughs as she responds. "You… you dumb shit. You want her, and you're like all the other men in Breakneck." She leans down to whisper. "You're all fucking pussies."

I clap my hands together like the smartass that I am. "Congratulations, you got us all figured out, don't you?"

"What's going on?"

I groan and turn towards my Prez. I'm that out of my game if I didn't even sense him enter the doctor's office. What in the fucking shit is wrong with me lately?

"Not shit. I'm outta here."

I'm going to fucking play. I have to get rid of all this excess frustration that has built up inside of me. If I can't release my demons, I might never get my shit back together. The thought makes me ill. I don't even wait for the Prez to give me orders. I'm not doing jack shit until after I sink my cock into some pussy.

"What's his fucking problem?" Prez asks Winter as I walk away.

"I was being nosey," she replies.

Damn straight, she was. I sense eyes on me as I leave, and this time I know where they are coming from. All these damn horny, pregnant women think I'm a prime steak that they want to sink their teeth into. Little do they know I'm the big bad wolf, and if anyone is going to sink some teeth into flesh, it'll be me. If the Prez thinks I'm coming back to this cesspool of little lambs, he's got another thing coming. I'd rather do the prospects' job and clean the damn toilets.

I wish I could straddle my lady right now, but since I had to drive Prez's wife around, I'm stuck with the fucking Rover. I could go back and get my metal, but that would waste time, and I desperately need to ease this itch that's clawing at me from the inside.

Once I'm in the Rover, I dig out my prepay and double-check my messages. I may say I need pussy right now, but if my brothers did call on me, I'd be there. Hands down, no questions asked. I press the button to light up my screen.

Nothing. Hell yes.

I throw my phone into the passenger seat, start up the Rover, and make my way to heaven. I look in the rearview mirror and smirk at myself.

Yeah, you're about to play, buddy.

***

When the doorman checks my membership, he eyes my gun, and I give him a look that says, try me. He steps aside for me to enter Euphoria. I don't even bother going to the bar to grab a quick drink. I'm not here for fucking chit chat. My sorry-ass friend Alec leans against his office door, his arms laced across his chest as he studies the crowd. I won't start a scene until I talk with him first. The asshole is so lax lately, I have to get information before I flag someone. The system of approach at this particular club is simple. Well, it would be if Alec hadn't grown so lazy.

It is imperative a person know the etiquette of the place where he or she is having a scene. Think of it like this. I can't walk up into someone's home and do as I want. I don't go in, thinking I know everything there is to know about the place, and prop my feet up on the damn coffee table. If I do something like that, I'll find my ass back out on the sidewalk.

Take the leather adorning my right wrist, for instance. One band signals that I'm a Dominant Sadist. The one with thin, light red stitching indicates that I like blood play. Alec's flagging system is as simple as it is tasteful, but again, he's becoming negligent.

"What's good?" I ask as I near him.

"Damn cops still hanging around." Alec turns towards me, frowning.

I would love nothing more than to say I told you so. I've warned him that he was getting too slack with the club. The kink world needs to stay locked tight like a fucking vault. People lose jobs because of this particular lifestyle. Not to mention, it's illegal almost everywhere.

"Sir..."

Before turning my attention towards Rose, Euphoria's manager, I slip into my persona. Alec has strict rules for her to call all club members Sir or Ma'am when addressing them. I give a little nod, gesturing her to continue.

"Your lease is up. Would you like to renew it?"

I hate to waste money, knowing the club is taking over, but if I don't renew, Alec will become suspicious. When it comes to my lifestyle, I am a creature of habit.

"Yes, thank you, Rose."

"Very well, Sir. Enjoy," she says quietly as she walks away.

I would love to play with her, but again, it is against the rules. Even if Alec were to become slack on that one, I wouldn't touch her. Although her long, red hair and blue eyes appeal to me, and her light, porcelain skin would look lovely with red marks, she's off limits to me.

"Still don't want to give up your room, eh?"

I take my attention from Rose's backside and turn back towards my friend.

"Month after month, you know me." I would hate for my room to go towards some dumb fuck who wouldn't tend to it properly. I have everything how I like it. My belongings are nicely organized and sterile, and I want to keep it that way. If I don't follow up on my lease, my shit will be stuck in a small locker, and what a pain in the ass that would become.

"You require Yolanda before you leave?" Alec questions.

I refrain from saying, "Don't I always," and nod yes.

Yolanda is a godsend here at Euphoria. Her job is to sterilize, organize, and clean everything with bleach. Some refuse to use her because her services are expensive. She is paid a salary for her basic duties, but when it comes to sterilizing toys and personalized rooms, she charges extra. It's Alec's way of getting her more money without him actually being the one to pay it. She deserves the extra, though.

Hell, if it weren't for her, and the fact that Rose is such a great manager, I wouldn't even play here anymore. I'd play at my house. With Rose in charge, I don't worry about STD screenings. She is on top of that. In all honesty, when Breakneck takes over this club, I plan to ask Winter and Prez if Rose and Yolanda can continue their employment here. It'd be a shame to lose them when they are very knowledgeable and discreet with this lifestyle.

"What are your tastes today, my friend?"

Hmm… "Rose has me yearning for a pale, redhead."

Alec looks around. "Right over there." He nods his head to the left. "Haven't had her, but I hear good things."

My eyes follow his line of sight until they reach the woman he is referring to. She'll do. Although her skin is pale, her red hair is definitely not natural. After I finish looking over her body, my eyes go to her left wrist and I smirk. Lovely little, fake redhead, I'm coming for you.

I don't bother with unnecessary goodbyes as I stalk my way over to her. I need to let some of this frustration loose, and as soon as possible. My demons claw at my chest cavity, begging for release. Her eyes roam my body and, stopping at the leather on my wrist, she nods in acceptance and puts her cigarette out. I don't wait for her. I don't have to. She'll follow. I stroll through the club with confident movements that would make most spectators weak in the knees. I'm a man on a mission.

As I get to my room and dig out my key, the fake redhead comes up behind me. No words are necessary as she waits for me to unlock the door. I nudge it open with my foot, using my hand to gesture her inside first. I am not a complete asshole. I still have some manners.

Once the door is shut and lockcd, I shrug out of my leather cut and walk over to the closet. I have no patience for clutter. Thankfully, I've learned to separate my club from my extra-curricular activities because, let's face it, some of my brothers are fucking disgusting. After hanging up my cut, I head towards the dresser.

"What shall I call you?" My hands slide along the cold, polished surface. I don't bother looking at her yet. I'm studying her to see if she is looking for an emotional connection with her scene mate.

"Sunny, Sir."

Good. So far, we are on the same page, but I don't like to be called Sir. "You'll address me as Tavis."

"Tavis." She repeats it slowly, making sure she gets it correct.

"Yes, Sunny. Tavis, not Travis." My fingers continue to slowly caress the wood. "Drop your skirt and kick it over."

The sound of her zipper sings in my ears and the demons inside me rustle about. I fling my shades off and dig the contact case out of my pocket. With my back to her, I pinch the blue lenses out of my eyes, and as I place them in their container, her leather skirt lands on the toe of one of my boots. I want her frightened, and what better way to accomplish that than showing her my soulless eyes. "Now, your corset."

"Yes, Tavis." She murmurs.

Her breathing picks up as I unbuckle my pants and toe off my boots and socks.

"Corset, Sunny." My stern voice spurs her to action. "The word is simple. That word is Red. Do you have a problem with that as a safe word?"

"Red is perfect," she breathes.

As I unbutton my black shirt, I ask her the necessary questions. "Hard limits. Go."

"Scat, caning, permanent body modification, fire, wax, and needle play are the basics of my hard limits."

Very good, I can work off that.

"Can I assume breath play is a soft limit?" I ask as I shrug from my shirt and place it neatly over the back of the couch.

"Yes, Tavis. For breath play, I usually respond better if my arousal is at a heightened state."

We could delve deeper into more limits, but these are the basics needed for an easy, quick scene.

"Pain tolerance, Sunny?" I plan to use a disposable pinwheel on her. My demons are itching to press the utensil down to trail red marks along that beautiful porcelain body. It is one of my preferred tools.

"About average, as long as I'm in a heightened state. I'll be fine, I assure you."

I trust no one that uses the term about average to describe pain levels, so I mark that on my mental checklist. I shuck off my jeans and her breath catches again. I don't wear boxers or briefs. Waste of time, those fuckers are. If I weren't about to do a scene, I'd chuckle at her wide-eyed expression. I turn towards her, finally giving her the opportunity to see all of me more clearly.

"Good. It's time I let my demons out to play," I snarl as I stalk towards her.

***

Chapter Four

Tatiana

I pull a burger wrapper from underneath my passenger seat. *Dammit, Piper!* She's always trashing my car. If I didn't love her free way of life, I'd bitch at her for this. I throw it in the trash bag and stick my head back against the floorboard as I lift the flashlight to shine it under the seat. Starburst wrappers, good god! Where does all this fattening crap show up on her? If I ate this much junk, I'd be a lard ass.

When one of my favorite songs plays on the radio, I reach up from the floorboard and turn the knob so it blares louder. When I pull a Snickers wrapper from under the seat, I reach into my cup holder for my phone and send her a text message while singing at the top of my lungs.

Me: 9:08 pm – Seriously!

Piper: 9:09 pm – U must b cleanin ur car out…

Me: 9:10 pm – uh yeah wtf Pipe!

Piper: 9:10 pm - *shrugs* whoopsy

Whoopsy? Freaking whoopsy? What is she twelve?

I throw my phone onto the seat and reach blindly for the bucket of soapy water sitting outside my car door. Once I grab a wet rag, I clean up the chocolate goo stuck to the track underneath my seat. I'm going to have to take my car and get it detailed. This is ridiculous.

And they say I'm the child. I think Piper takes the cake on this one.

Someone kicking my feet startles me out of my inner bitchfest. Before I look, I already know who it is. I take a deep breath in, slowly let it out, and then reach to turn the volume down on my radio. Scooting backwards out of the car, when my feet touch the ground, I stand and look at him.

"Whatcha doin', darlin'?"

Why does his thick southern drawl have to sound so damn delicious?

"Cleaning up after Piper." I toss the wet rag in the bucket, and the soapy water swishes back and forth against the sides.

"She is a force to be reckoned with." He chuckles and I smirk.

That is a nice way of saying she is a tornado, but before I can find myself happy about the reason for this little chit chat, I get a whiff of pure sex sweat. The smile evaporates from my face as quickly as it came.

"Go shower, Shadow. You smell like a two dollar hooker," I grumble as I turn my attention back to my car.

"What the fuck is wrong with you? We can't even talk now without you insulting me. Shit used not to be this way with us, Tea."

I pivot back towards him with a scowl. "Nothing is wrong with me. You stink something awful. If you want to smell like a cheap lay, that's on you."

Shadow lifts his sunglasses to the top of his head, and I almost want to yell at him for wearing them at dusk. But when I notice his contacts are out, I stop myself. Very few times can I see into Shadow's soul, and I'm not about to say something that will make him slide the glasses down and cut me out in the process.

"We used to be friends. What the fuck happened, Tea?"

My blue eyes search his soulless ones and I come to realize he's hurt. He is actually upset that I've been standoffish. The thought makes my chest ache. He's been nothing but good to me, and I've been nothing but an ass. He can't help it that I am severely attracted to him, no more than he can help the way he is.

"I'm sorry. I'll try to be less of a bitch from now on."

He tries to move in for a hug and I swat at him.

"No way, dude. Go shower first." I force a laugh even though it rips my heart apart to know that he just finished screwing someone else.

"Shit, sorry babe." He chuckles as he turns and heads towards the live-in building.

I really need to go home, but Dad won't allow it because of club business. All I want is to cry in my own damn bed until I fall asleep.

"Hey sis, what's up?" Mace hops onto the trunk of my car.

Jesus, they're coming out of the woodwork tonight.

"You dent my car, you're paying to un-dent it."

He swings his legs back and forth like a child while he tongues a toothpick back and forth between his lips. "Let's go grab a burger. I'll buy."

Bonding time with my new brother is something I am always up for having. "Let me call Dad. I'm not supposed to leave the compound without an escort."

31

Mace is prospecting, so Dad should approve. I reach into my car, grab my cell phone, and dial his number. Not only will I get time with my brother, but I will also get out of this club for a bit. Dad answers on the first ring.

"What's wrong, Tatiana?" He chuckles as Storm whispers in the background.

Oh gross, please tell me I didn't call him during that shit. I rush to get my question out.

"Can Mace take me for a burger?"

I hear more whispering before I get my answer.

"To Ma and Pop's, then get your asses back to the compound." As I start to hang-up the phone, he shocks me. "Thanks for calling and asking, baby girl, instead of doin'."

Ah hell, my dad is getting all sweet. "Uh, no problem, Dad." I click off and stare at my phone for a moment.

"That was weird. He said yes, but we have to go to Ma and Pop's restaurant. Let's walk, so it takes longer," I say as I take the keys out of my car, reach for my purse, and then shut the door.

"I'm still new around here and shit, but you tend to do just about whatever you want to do, sis." Mace laughs as he hops off my trunk.

He's right.

"You're maturing, little sis," he jokes playfully as he slugs my shoulder.

"Fuck off." I laugh, even though I know he's onto something.

When we come to the gate, Rap wheels himself over. The poor

guy only has a few more weeks left in that wheelchair. "You guys going for food?"

I nod. "Yeah, burgers, you want something?"

Rap mumbles yes and digs his wallet out of the doggy bag that hangs from the back of his chair. He hates it, but he doesn't have the heart to tell Storm to take it off. She feels guilty about his broken legs, and when he was cursing nonstop about how he couldn't even lift his ass to piss or get his wallet out, they came up with his doggy bag. Storm and Winter even put temporary rails in the bathroom so the man could lift himself. "I gave the prospects a night off of gate duty because I fuckin' can't do anything else right now and it's driving me fuckin' nuts," he grumbles as he hands me a twenty. "Where you goin' for the burgers?"

I take the money from him as Mace tells him Ma and Pop's.

"Thank fuck. Okay, you know my usual, then, right, Darlin'?"

An honest to god laugh bubbles from my throat. "Rap, I know you all so well, I can tell each of you when you're going to shit, before you even know it."

I'm not kidding, either. Since I've spent all my life around the club and haven't had anything else to do but watch people, I've memorized their patterns, whether I wanted to or not.

Rap's smile is blinding as he hits the gate button. I'm sad for him. He finished prospecting not too long ago, and he's been stuck in that damn chair for months. I know he is itching to do club stuff, but he's been patient about it all, except for his little tirade about pissing and stuff.

"Take your time, little Tea. I know your dad has had you on a short leash. My stomach isn't rumbling yet."

I lean down and peck him on his cheek. "For that, I'll bring you back a chocolate shake, my treat."

"After my heart, I see," he teases as Mace and I walk out.

"See you in a bit, Rap." I wave goodbye.

***

While Mace and I wait for our order, we chat about his upbringing, and how it pisses him off we didn't grow up together. It shocks me how open he is emotionally. He's not afraid of his feelings or of expressing them, and I admire him for that.

"So, do you think Dad and Storm will try for kids again one day?" Mace asks while the waitress places our food on the table. Before she walks away, I give her Rap's to-go order, and then turn my attention back to my brother's question.

"I honestly don't know. Her pregnancy was a shock, and Dad didn't even know about it until she was miscarrying. She was actually on her way to tell him," I mumble around a giant bite of the juicy hamburger.

"It's fuckin' sad," Mace says before slurping his Coca Cola.

See, not afraid to admit emotions. Breakneck needs more men like my brother.

"It is," I agree. "Even though she's only a few years older than us, she has that motherly feel already."

I dip a fry into my chocolate shake.

"Is that any good?" my brother asks.

"Really good. Here try it." I push my shake towards him. "Rap actually got me addicted to doing it. That's why I told him I'd bring him one. That reminds me. We should probably go to the corner store and get him some smokes and rolling papers, too. He doesn't like asking people to do stuff for him."

Mace dips a few fries into the chocolate goodness and shoves them into his mouth. "That is so fucking good." He groans.

"Yeah, it is." I smile at him.

"So, you really do know all the brothers well." He dips more fries into my shake. My heart squeezes when I realize how comfortable we are around one another.

"I do. Rap is one of my favorites, because of our ages being so close. Well... now I have a new favorite," I tease as I steal my shake back.

"I'm your favorite now?" he says as he takes a bite out of his giant burger.

"Of course, you are. You're my brother, my twin. I always felt like I was missing a piece of myself until you came along a few months ago. Now I know why," I say as I shy away. I don't want to scare him off.

"I get what you're saying. It's gotta be that weird twin shit."

Oh good. I didn't freak him out. "So you felt it too?"

He nods. "Yeah, and being adopted didn't help. It's probably why I was the black sheep."

I don't know what to say. I'm pissed off at the useless woman who gave birth to us for even giving him up in the first place. The only thing that keeps me from going to her and strangling the hell out of her is that my brother had good adoptive parents.

"I don't know what to say, Mace."

His shoulders shrug as he finishes off his last bite. "They're good people. It ended up being okay, sis, honest. It was a good life."

I fight to smile. "And now you're here."

"And now I'm here, where I belong."

Mace pays our bill, and even pays for Rap's order, so I shove the twenty back in my pocket and decide to use it on his smokes and rolling papers. I tip the waitress even though Mace protests, and I tell him it is the least I could do after him buying me dinner.

We talk about how he used to race street bikes and get into all kinds of trouble with his adoptive parents. He says he'll always love them, and will check up on them, and even visit them every few holidays, but as far as he is concerned, he belongs here.

When we get to the corner store, Mace buys his smokes and I wait behind him.

"Well, hello, Tatiana. Don't you two look alike," Donald says as he eyes my brother and me up and down.

"About that… he's my twin. You know how the bitch is." I shrug. Everyone in town knows my mother if they're close to her age. She was a slut back then and probably still is. "Rap's usual, please."

"You got it, suga'." Donald smiles at me. "Oh, before I forget, can you let Braxxon know the club order came in? Save me the phone call."

I nod. I'm surprised someone hasn't picked up the alcohol delivery yet. They're usually on that like clockwork. I shoot Braxxon a text so I don't forget to let him know.

Me: 10:37 pm - @ Don's, orders n

Not a minute passes before he replies.

Godfather: 10:37 pm – Send prospects n mornin' it's late daughter

"Godfather," Mace asks from behind me.

I laugh. "Yeah, your new Prez is my Godfather. If something happens to Dad, he'll take care of me. Don, Braxxon will send some prospects in the morning. This knucklehead will probably be one of them." I gesture to Mace with my cell phone as I type a reply.

Me: 10:39 pm – I know, Mace is w/ me, headed home

Godfather: 10:40 pm – k

After I pay for Rap's stuff, we say our goodbyes and head back to the compound. I thank Mace on the way for getting me out of there. I can leave whenever I want, but I'd rather not stress my dad or Braxxon out too much right now. When we get back, Rap lets us in the gate. Mace hands him his food as I dig his smokes, papers, and change out of my purse.

"Mace bought us dinner, so I figured I'd use your money for smokes and papers," I say as I put it all in his doggy bag.

"Good call. Thanks, you two," he says as we walk away.

Mace and I say our goodbyes and part ways when we get to the home building. The lights are off, and if it weren't a weekday, I'd wonder why everything is so quiet tonight. Everyone that's awake must be over in the clubhouse. The warm food in my stomach has made me sleepy and with no energy left, I slowly trudge up the stairs to my floor. When I reach the landing, I am relieved. I unlock my door, go in, and flop onto my bed while I kick off my shoes. It has been the longest day of my life today. I've caught up on homework, got to know my brother more, and dealt with Shadow on two separate occasions. I'm wiped.

***

Chapter Five

Shadow

As I smoke my cigarette in the dark at the picnic table, I can't help but grin as Tatiana comes in with her brother. She looks happy right now, and I haven't seen that smile of hers in forever. Most of the time, it's forced. This one, however, is natural and real, and it's the most beautiful thing I've ever seen.

I watch her after she gives Rap his food, and she walks into the main building. When she looks like that, I find it extremely difficult to keep my eyes off of her. I put out my smoke as my Prez comes out of the clubhouse.

"She looked happy," he says as he sits next to me.

"Were you watching her or somethin'?" I ask.

He nods. "She sent me a text from Don's. I wanted to make sure she got back in okay."

The protection around Tea is extreme, and she wonders why I won't let my demons loose on her.

"She's only my goddaughter, and yet it makes me ill to the fuckin' stomach, brother, to think of something happenin' to her," he grumbles as he lights up a joint. "I can't smoke this shit up in my room around Winter, so I'm getting it outta the way before heading up there."

I'm in agreement with that. It pisses me off when people do drugs around pregnant women or children. "Think you'll have your own to worry about soon enough."

He puffs and then passes the joint to me. "Yeah, if her

hormones don't kill me first, man. I shit you not, sometimes I think she's possessed." He whispers the last word.

"Afraid Winter might hear ya, Prez?" I chuckle.

"Fuck yeah, I'm afraid. You haven't seen what this pregnancy is doing to her," he mock whispers.

I don't say anything to that. She seems like the same Winter I've known since I arrived.

"You can finish that off, brother. I got a wife to fuck."

I put the joint in my mouth and stand as he does so we can bro-pat, and then I walk to the clubhouse. I'm exhausted, but I don't want to be alone with my thoughts. When the door slams shut behind me, I hear laughing.

"Sniper, that isn't how you play pool," Piper chastises before she sees me coming down the hall. "Hey, Shadow, can I get a hit off that?"

I puff one more time, long and hard, because I won't get it back once Sniper gets a hold of it, and then I pass it to her.

"I can play pool how the fuck ever I wanna play pool. What are you, the pool referee?"

She smacks him with her free hand as the other brings the weed up to her mouth. "No, but shit, you're never serious," she says as she puffs.

I roll my eyes.

"You're never serious, is she, Shadow?" Sniper brings me in on it, and I think what the hell. I need to have some entertainment.

"He's got you, Pipe. A few hours ago, Tea was digging all your stash trash out of her car. You're free as a bird, darlin'," I

40

respond.

"I may be free, but I know that the white ball doesn't go into the damn holes," she grumbles.

Sniper and I laugh as we both say, "Cue ball."

She throws her pool stick up onto the table, huffing as she flops down on the sofa. "Whatever."

"Ah, babe, don't be like that." Sniper laughs as he flops down next to her.

I'll never understand those two. We all wonder if Sniper and Piper are fucking and not telling anyone about it.

I walk behind the bar as he continues trying to get her to stop sulking.

"I have something that'll make you feel better, Piper." I chuckle as I get the ingredients for bomb pops out. All the women here love them.

"Bomb pops," she squeals.

"Mhmm, get your sulking ass over here, and I'll make you a few."

My eyebrows pull together when I can't find the grenadine. I'm searching high and low for that shit when the door slams and in comes Pyro. He takes one look at the ingredients on the counter and knows what I'm looking for. He holds up one finger as he says, "make me one," and opens the top cabinet, revealing a bottle of the red liquid. As I pour enough to get us all hammered, the door slams again, and in walks Tatiana looking fucking hot as hell in her small shorts, tank top, and slippers. Oh hell, this is going to be a long night.

"Make me one," she grumbles. "I couldn't sleep. Messed up

41

part is that I'm exhausted, too."

Sit the fuck down, Tea! Get those fine ass legs out of my goddamn view!

"Tatiana!" Piper squeals and engulfs her.

Tea looks from me to Sniper, to Pyro, trying to figure out if Piper's drunk yet. When we all shrug, Tea pats her on the back.

"Piper, you take some happy pills again?" Tea jokes.

"Hell yeah, I did. Want one?"

Jesus Christ! Tea on drugs? Fuck no, no way, not happening. Over my dead body.

Pyro and Sniper seem to have the same thoughts as I do, and we try to snatch the little white pill away from Piper as she hands it off to Tea. We're too late. Tatiana snatches it up and slips it into her mouth faster than our arms can move.

"Too late." She giggles as her mouth hangs open and she moves her tongue up and down. I groan quietly, imagining what that tongue could do to my cock.

"Your dad is gonna fuckin' kill me, baby girl," Pyro says in frustration.

"You didn't see shit, so, therefore, you don't say shit, Uncle Pyro."

He curses some more before calming himself. "I may not be your blood, but I'm still your uncle, as you said, and fuck am I pissed at you!"

I don't even want to think about what ZZ or Prez will do if they find out about this shit.

"Come on, I'm around family. Nothing will happen to me here.

Let me live a little bit, please," she begs.

The pleading tone in her voice makes us all relax a little. She is stuck here all the damn time, and she didn't get to party much growing up.

"And where the fuck are the rest of your clothes," Pyro roars out of the blue.

I want a fucking answer to that question, as well.

"I'm in my pajamas and I'm at home. Are you trying to tell me that I can't wear my pajamas around the club? Are you trying to give me more damn rules to follow?" she argues as her hand lands on her hip.

When she puts it like that, it even makes me feel like a fucking asshole. This club traps her enough. She has enough rules to follow and never gets to live. She's starving to be free. Piper comes up behind her and runs her fingers through Tea's hair. Oh no, oh, fuck no.

"Pipe," I glare at her hard, "what did you give Tea?" Only one little white pill makes people touchy-feely and is easily found around these parts. I have a bad feeling.

"Ecstasy, duh!"

We all groan as Piper and Tea smile at one another.

"C'mon, Sniper. We got our graves to go and dig," Pyro grumbles.

We are so fucking dead. ZZ and Prez are going to kill us. This can't be happening. We don't need this shit right now. And I especially don't want to be around a horny Tatiana. Oh, fuck no.

"Come on, stop overreacting. At least I'm trying it here, around people I can trust. Let me live a little, please! Stop treating me like I'm a child. I'm not a little girl anymore." She gestures to her appearance.

No, she definitely is not a little girl.

Sniper and Pyro whisper together before finally reaching a conclusion about the situation.

"Drink lots of water tonight. We're not leaving your side, and if anything starts to go wrong, we're telling your dad and the Prez."

I thought that Tea would squeal or shout in happiness over winning the situation, but instead, she nods in agreement with them. This is going to be the longest fucking night of my life. If I could drag myself away from this, I would, but I can't. I'm going to be worried about her until this shit wears off. So I do the only thing I can do. I finish making the drinks and prepare myself.

***

About 90 minutes later…

The music is cranked as loud as the clubhouse speakers go, and the giggling from Piper and Tatiana is giving me a fucking migraine. The three of us, me, Sniper, and Pyro, are sitting on the couch, and I'm trying to stay sober between each shot. I don't want to get so drunk that I'll be too fucked up to help if something goes wrong.

"Dammit, baby girl, drink some more water," Pyro growls as he shoves a bottle into the air, waiting for her to dance by and grab it.

"Nothing compares toooo…" Tatiana sings out as she dances over to the water. "Rock and Roll, baby," she croons over the top of the bottle 'microphone.'

She tilts the bottle to her lips, guzzling the water, and some of it trickles down her neck. I gulp. This is too much. Way too fucking much. Her blonde curly hair piled on top of her head bounces as she dances around. When the bottle finally comes down, I think thank fuck as she puts it on the table in front of us. But no, she couldn't make it that easy for me. She raises her tank up beneath her tits so I can see her rock hard abs. I throw my head back and rub my forehead. I swear, it makes me want to toss Piper over my knees and spank the shit out of her for making me go through this with Tatiana.

"It's so fucking hot," Tatiana cries, forcing my attention back to her.

She picks up the bottle again, dumping the rest of the water over her head. She should look stupid doing this, but she doesn't. She looks like a wet dream as the water cascades down her sweaty body.

"She's fuckin' killin' me," I grumble. "This is too much. Oh, god."

"It's killin' you? Motherfucker, that's our fuckin' niece, brother," Pyro whisper yells.

"You! Piper never acts like this," Sniper growls angrily. "I'm gonna fucking spank her for this shit tomorrow."

Goddammit, Sniper!

Now I'm thinking about taking Tatiana over my fucking knee. God's getting me back for shit. That's it. That's what this shit is. I throw my head into my hands before reaching for another shot.

* * *

30 minutes later…

Pyro laughs his ass off as both Tatiana and Piper suffocate us with attention.

"Why don't you like me, Shadow? Am I not pretty enough for you?" Tatiana laughs from my lap.

I swear to hell and back, I'm going to punch Pyro for thinking this is funny. Nothing is amusing about Tea sitting in my lap, laughing and rubbing her sweaty, half-naked body all over me. This situation is fucking serious!

"Yeah, Sniper, am I not pretty enough for you?" Piper giggles beside me.

These two are fucking playing off of one another.

Unfuckingbelievable!

"Shadow," she breathes against my mouth, and my eyes fly back towards her. "Answer me."

Shit! Get that beautiful mouth away from me, Tea, baby, please! I beg silently.

When her small, delicate hands reach to tilt my shades up, I panic. She can't see inside me. She can't fucking read how bad I want her right now, and it takes every ounce of my self-control to keep from throwing her onto the table and fucking the shit out of her. The only thing stopping me is that she's fucked up, and I have morals. FUCK! But when my shades come off, she slowly puts them on her face, and dammit, she actually looks more beautiful, if that's possible. I smirk at her. I rarely smile, grin, or laugh, but at this moment, she makes me want to do all of those things.

"How do I look?" She giggles, bouncing her ass against my dick.

Another groan escapes me as I answer her. "Hot, Tea, fucking hot."

"Thank you." She smiles big enough to light up the room. She is quiet for a moment as she contemplates what next to say, and instead of words, her mouth comes down onto mine. Instead of pushing her away, I growl into her mouth and my hands clamp down on her bare thighs. As her tongue probes my bottom lip, Pyro's voice brings me back to the present.

"Brother…"

Yeah, yeah, fuck! I know she's fucked up. It takes everything in me to tear my lips away from hers. Tatiana won't have it though, and her hands fly up to hold my face still as her tongue pushes into my mouth.

Oh, fuck!

My fingers dig into her skin as she sucks on my tongue. No woman has ever kissed me like this. As my body heats, I growl into her mouth and take control. She wants to kiss? I'll fucking give her all I've got. I clutch her thighs once more before my hands fly to her hips and I shift her so she's straddling me. One hand slides up to hold the back of her neck and squeezes tightly as my other hand grips the globes of her ass and my tongue assaults hers. I suck and bite at her until she's gasping for breath. When Pyro snarls, I slow my attack and ease her back down.

The couch squeaks, and out of the corner of my eye, I see Sniper fling Piper back onto the pool table, her legs wrapped tightly around him. Interesting.

Tatiana squeezes her legs against my thighs, pressing her pussy against my jeans to draw my attention back to her.

My head glides to the side and I beg Pyro with my eyes to fucking help me. I only have so much strength.

He chuckles as he stands and lifts Tea from my lap, and I sigh in relief, shocked to find my cock is almost fucking hard. I look down at my lap and frown. That's never fucking happened before.

Huh.

"Seems my niece has a wild side," he says as he fights against a wiggling Tea.

No shit!

I can't even process what the fuck has happened. Not only did I fucking kiss Tatiana, but my dick fucking almost got hard without me causing her any pain. That hasn't happened since I was a teen.

***

A few hours later…

Tatiana is once again in my lap, and for the first time I can ever remember, I'm wiped out from doing nothing. Worrying about her all night, and fighting for my dear life to keep her from raping me, has been exhausting as hell, and my eyes fight to stay open as I hold her. I don't know where Piper and Sniper took off to, but it quieted down after they left.

"Let me sleep here," she mumbles as the high wears off.

I push the sweaty strands of hair away from her face, relieved I have my glasses back to hide my eyes so I can stare at her. She's so fucking beautiful, and it makes me ache all over. For the first time since meeting her, I wish I could have her, if only once, without paying a price for it. Tatiana is the kind of girl that'll develop too much emotion, and I can't hurt her. I won't. Yes, the irony is not lost on me as I think that. I mean I can't hurt her emotionally. She's too good for all my troubled bullshit.

"She's something special, isn't she?" Pyro yawns beside me.

"Priceless." Sighing, I look over at him with my walls down.

He tries to fight off his smile. "I'm headed to bed. You good?"

She's fucking wiped out, coming off a high she's never experienced before, and Pyro knows her well enough to know if it is safe for us all to sleep.

"I'm good," I reply as he stands and lays his jacket over a sleeping Tatiana.

"Night, brother," he says before yawning again and walking away.

I let out a breath and tilt my head to the side.

You're not going to make this easy on me, are you, darlin'?

When she stirs and wiggles closer to my chest, I realize this is going to be the hardest thing I've ever done in my fucking life. Denying her is going to be so damn painful.

***

Chapter Six

Shadow

Something kicks me awake, and now, I am straight up pissed off. I was sleeping hard, too. Nothing could prepare me for a steaming hot ZZ and a laughing Storm holding a tray of coffee, standing in front of me, though. Fuck a flying duck. I throw my hands in the air when I realize they are still gripping Tea's ass, and whisper, "Nothing happened," as I deposit her onto the couch and stand.

"Nothing happened," he yells.

I shush him as I look over my shoulder to make sure he didn't wake her.

"Other than her attacking my mouth, no, nothing happened. She did Ecstasy last night, and a few of us stayed up with her until she came down."

Storm swallows her laugh and gulps when she sees ZZ's jaws flex.

"Who gave her the X?"

He isn't about to turn me into a fucking rat. He knows better. What the hell!

"You know it was Piper, so don't even get like that," Storm chastises.

Hey, as long as that shit didn't come out of my mouth.

ZZ sighs his aggravation as he bends down to pick her up off the couch. Tatiana nuzzles against his shoulder as her sleepy eyes crack open.

"I did Ecstasy last night, Daddy," she whispers.

Storm can't hold her laughter any longer, and her body shakes uncontrollably as she lets it fly.

"I'm daddy right now, huh?" he says as he kisses her forehead.

"I'm sorry, I won't do it again. I feel like hell," she mumbles.

I bet she feels like hell. I never pray, but I want to. I want to pray that she remembers absolutely none of this. But something deep in my gut tells me I won't be so lucky, when she peeks over at me as ZZ turns to walk her out.

"Attacked your mouth, huh?" Storm asks as she hands me a coffee.

I don't reply until I've gulped down half the scalding cup of Jo and light up a smoke. It's way too damn early to be answering 101 questions, but seeing as she cares about Tatiana as much as I do, I'll tell her.

"Yeah, it was something else," I murmur as I take another drag from my cig.

"You're lucky ZZ trusts you with her, or I have a feeling that might've been a lot worse than it was."

Yeah, no shit.

He shouldn't trust me with her, though. That's the fucking problem, but he can't grasp that concept.

Storm takes the hint that I'm finished discussing last night with her. In fact, I don't ever want to speak of it again. It was so beyond messed up, and I can't even begin to explain it. With everything that happened, I don't know what to think. Hell, I'm not sure if I even know which way is up or down.

My legs are stiff as I walk out of the clubhouse towards the main building. A cold shower calls to me. It'll help straighten out my foggy, muddled head. One thing I don't like is being confused about shit. Life isn't supposed to be simple, but I do all that I can to make it that way. And Tatiana is doing anything but making my life simple right now. She's fucking it all up with her blonde curly hair, blue eyes as bright as the sky, and her toned body that could last for hours restrained with rope.

Fuck me!

It is official. I fucking want her, and now, I have to find a way to keep me from taking what I need. I have never once denied myself anything I desire. I take that shit without looking back, and now, I am about to see how solid my restraint actually is. One problem with that, though, is Tatiana tests my control more than I test myself, which is two devils working as one against me.

When I reach my room, I head straight for the bathroom, turn on the cold water, and strip down. Thinking about Tatiana tied up for hours, with rope cutting into her delicate wrists, has me rock fucking hard.

When the cold spray hits my hot skin, I place one hand against the wall, wrap my other hand around my cock, and tighten my fingers as I pull. Her mouth on mine replays over and over in my head with each tug of my wrist, jerking my cock up and down. I crave more, so I imagine her mouth on me, her hands bound behind her back, as her head bobs up and down. Her tongue slurps against my skin as I wrap my hands in her hair and yank hard. The image is enough to tighten my balls, and my swimmers shoot out under the stream of water. I rest my forehead against the shower wall as my breathing steadies and the icy water cascades down my body.

I'm so fucked when it comes to her, and I am so damn confused. She's all up in my head, and she doesn't even know it. When I can finally breathe easy, I stand straight, grab a washcloth, and spread soap onto it. My mind has somewhat cleared by the time my prepay rings with Prez's ringtone.

Fuck, yes, some fucking normalcy back in my life.

***

We sit around the table in church, shooting the shit while waiting for Sniper to show. Prez looks at his watch, lights up a smoke, and curses under his breath in irritation. ZZ hasn't said another word to me about last night, and I'm fucking stoked. I hope to god he hasn't said shit to the Prez, either.

Ten minutes later, Sniper finally graces us with his presence.

"Brother, you put your make-up on or something?" Prez barks.

Sniper growls as he slams the door behind him and takes a seat. Hidden behind my shades, I close my eyes, because, judging by his looks, I can tell he's about to bring up last night.

"I was up late."

You motherfucking ass prick!

"I don't give a fuck if you haven't slept in a week. When I call church, your ass needs to be here on time. Max, take away his cut for a week," Prez orders.

"Prez," Max says in acknowledgment.

"I'm not even gonna argue with you right now, Prez. Take it away, whatever," he says as he lights up a cig.

We groan. He knows better than to fucking talk to the Prez like that, no matter if he's blood or not. What the hell is he thinking?

"Two fucking weeks, Max. Keep going, brother. Blood or not, I'm about to shoot your ass in the fuckin' kneecaps," Prez growls as he slams the gavel down against the wooden plank.

Sniper says nothing while he inhales his nicotine and then blows it out in Prez's face.

"Pushing it, Sniper. You're fuckin' pushing it!"

Prez looks around the table for any more fuckers about to get lippy with him, but we all sit quietly. Sniper must be real hungover if he is disrespecting not only his patch, position, and Prez, but also his blood brother. I don't even want to ask what happened between him and Piper. I honestly never wanted to before, but this proves I really don't want to know. It must have been as bad as my night was.

"Anyfuckinwho, this shit with the Chinese happens tomorrow afternoon. I've called a sitdown. Believe it or not, the leader or whatever the fuck he is, sounded more American over the phone than he did Chinese. That means I won't require a translator, so we can rule out that cost. Mr. Wong seemed very interested in our wanting to meet with him. Everyone in this club better respect him. Respect his position like you'd respect mine. You are to address him as Mr. Wong, and nothing fuckin' else. Is that clear?"

Grumbles erupt around the table. We hate bowing down or showing respect to those we don't know, and especially to those who haven't earned it.

"All right, Sniper, your ass better lose this attitude you got goin' on by tomorrow. You're goin'. Pyro, Shadow, and Smokey, as well. Max, ZZ, Rob, and Hammer, I want your asses around the block with your ladies roaring in case this doesn't roll smoothly. The rest of you are staying here with the family on lockdown. Not a fucking soul who doesn't have a club patch leaves this compound without my say so. Understood?"

Acknowledgment passes through the room and the gavel slams down.

***

Chapter Seven

Tatiana

When I wake up, I feel like a semi has run over me. The pounding in my skull makes me think my brain is going to fly out of my head at any moment and kill me. My feet hit the carpet as I lower them from the bed and the softness of the plush floor feels like a heaven-sent cushion to my sore body.

Never again, and that's that.

The night replays in my head, and I all but scream over what I can remember. I made a complete ass of myself. How am I supposed to face Shadow now? Oh, please wake up from this nightmare, Tatiana.

Jesus, my only hope is that he was drunk enough not to remember my behavior. It's no wonder he looks at me as if I'm a kid. It is because I act like one. I know better than to do that stuff.

Why, oh, why did I do this to myself?

On top of being miserable, I feel like the world's most childish woman. And, do I remember my dad carrying me to bed?

Oh, shit. I'm dead. Yep. No way is he going to allow me to get away with something as dumb as trying Ecstasy. My dad has only one rule. No drugs, and I broke that last night. Shit!

When I see my phone on the side table, I'm certain my dad put me to bed. This keeps getting worse. I grab it and send a text to Storm, asking how much trouble I am in.

Me: 2:23 pm – How much trouble???

Is it really after two in the afternoon? Holy crap, I lost half the day.

Storm: 2:24 pm – Not much, prob lecture

Probably? That doesn't ease my nerves in the least.

I need to take a shower and then get things settled with my dad. I don't want to hide from him. I'd rather get it over and done with.

***

I watch my dad clean his bike with a rag, chewing my lip as I build the courage to walk over and talk with him. I'm about to turn around and run away, when he spots me.

"Get over here, baby girl."

My feet seem to weigh a hundred pounds. With each step closer to him, it feels like I'm using every ounce of strength I have to take the next one.

"I'm sorry, Dad. I am. It was so stupid, and I regret it." My words rush out of my mouth.

Dad throws the rag into the bucket and pulls me into a hug, squeezing me so tight that I almost have to gasp for my next breath.

"Don't ever do that shit again, T. I'm serious. What if something would have happened to you?" he mumbles into my hair.

Oh, god. Now I feel even worse. He's worried, not angry.

"I swear on everything, I won't do that ever again," I say as I squeeze him back.

When he pulls back from me, he grasps my cheeks in his large hands, studies my face, and lets me see the pain laced in his eyes.

"You can drink, T, but no drugs, okay?"

I bring my hands up to my dad's arms and rub them, trying to comfort him. I've never seen him like this. It guts me.

"I got it. I'm pretty sure I made an ass out of myself, and the way I feel right now? This is not something I want to go through again. Lesson learned the hard way."

He seems satisfied with my answer and drops his hands from my cheeks.

"Winter was looking for you. She's in the clubhouse."

"I love you, Dad."

His face lights up. "I love you, too, kiddo, but don't fuckin' scare your old man like that again, okay?"

I cross my heart before walking towards the old building. I make a mental note to bake my dad some chocolate chip cookies, or at least go buy some. It has been our thing for as long as I can remember. When we're upset or mad at one another, chocolate chip cookies are our medium.

The oppressive heat outside only makes my awful hangover worse. As I open the door, and the chilled air from inside the building hits me, I feel a million times better.

I spot Winter at the bar wiping the counter down.

"You were looking for me?" I say as I sit on a barstool.

"I was. How you feeling?"

Oh, god. It's already making the rounds. I lay my face on the counter and groan. I'll never live this down now. I should have stayed in bed until tomorrow. The way drama goes around this place, my story would have been old news by then.

"Crap," I respond, the words muffled against the wood.

"I bet." She chuckles as she lifts my head with her hands. "You look like it, too."

Gee, thanks, friend.

"How did the appointment go?" I ask, trying to change the subject.

Her mouth tilts up. "It was good, heartbeat was good, and doc said the baby looked healthy, but it was still too soon to see the gender."

My skin prickles and my body heats. I know he's behind me before I even hear him. Shit, fuck, dammit!

I don't turn or say a word as he walks around the bar, opens the fridge, and grabs a Coke. This is so damn awkward. His nose is pointed in my direction, but I can't tell if he is looking at me, because he has on those damn shades.

I pretend to ignore him, even though every inch of me is aware of his presence. The hiss of the canned drink opening echoes loudly in my ears, and I imagine my senses going nuts because they are so focused and trained on him. A few moments pass, and the can flies across my line of vision, landing in the trash. My shoulders slump when my body senses he is gone.

"What the hell was that all about," Winter whispers.

Thank god, she didn't announce that sooner. I shake my head in a 'don't ask' manner. I thought she would have known, but seeing as she doesn't, I'm not about to share my humiliation with her. It is beyond embarrassing, and not something I want to keep on reliving.

***

Day two of ignoring Shadow

While I sit in the courtyard with my laptop and go over my lessons for the week, he comes out of the clubhouse. I immediately advert my attention, but he walks closer. I plead silently for him to keep on going, but, when I think I am free, he makes a sharp turn and sits down across from me at the picnic table.

My heart thumps against my chest, my breathing picks up, and I all but have a panic attack with him right freaking there.

"You mad at me?" he drawls in that deep southern voice.

Oh, god, no. Why would I be mad at him? I am the one who made a complete ass out of myself the other night. I shake my head no, not wanting to look up at him. I can't form any words that would not be considered babble. It is bad enough he already tells me I act like a child, but now, he's seen me do things that back up his malicious words.

"Okay… then the problem is…"

Please, don't do this, Shadow. Please, don't, I plead inside my head.

"Look, Tea, if this is about the other night? No worries. We're friends. We're cool."

His words repeat in my head before I dare to look up at him. "We're good? You're not mad?"

He shakes his head in disbelief. "Why would I be fuckin' mad at you, Tea?"

I stare at him with shock laced across my face. I practically hurled myself at him, if my memory serves me correctly. Maybe he is ignoring it. I mean, he did say no worries about the other night. My palms sweat and my knee bounces underneath the picnic table as I replay every single word he said. When I am finally happy with my conclusion that he doesn't want to relive it either, I finally speak. "Okay," I say in a quiet voice.

Shadow glares at me for a minute in his sexy way, before pushing his sunglasses to the top of his head so that he can peer directly into my soul. What is he trying to say, and what more does he want me to say? I don't understand this new development. Why, all of a sudden, is he showing me his eyes, at least more so than before? He doesn't even have his contacts in.

"I'm gonna lay it to you straight here, Tea. Yes, the other night was completely fucked up. You were fucked up! You all but dry humped my ass with your tongue down my throat. I'm not pissed, because I tongued your hot, sweet ass right back, but that shit can't happen again. I won't let it. I won't let my demons destroy you. You think you're into the shit that I am, and I know you're curious about it, but it. WILL. NEVER. HAPPEN."

My throat seizes and I gasp for air. I more than made an ass out of myself. I gave him reason, once again, to talk to me like this. Talk to me as if I don't know what the hell I am getting into with him. That boils the blood running through my veins to a degree I have never felt before. How dare him. He is beyond pushing my buttons now. He can only refer to me as a child in so many words before I will eventually snap, and by god, he's finally gone and done it. He's finally made me hate him!

I stand, and before I give myself time to think, I spew my angry words at him. "Don't you ever fucking talk to me again! You keep treating me like a goddamn child." I huff out. "How is this for acting like one? Let's play the silent game." I clench my fists and my cheeks heat up with anger. I catch my breath and whisper my final blow. "You see me, you turn the other way. I come into a room, you leave that room. You may wear that patch right there," I bend down and flick it, "but I have something you don't. I have a daddy that'll kill for me. How's that for childish?" I stomp my feet, cross my arms and stick out my tongue to further my so called childish behavior. "Huh? Your brotherhood ain't got shit on fatherhood. You fuck with me, and I'll tell my good old daddy on your ass. I'll show you a fucking child, you pompous prick."

With that, I spin on my heels and stomp away. I might as well play the part he has not so graciously given me. I wish I could see his not so smug face right now, but I refuse to turn around and look.

***

Chapter Eight

Shadow

I didn't sleep for shit last night. Tatiana's words kept playing over and over in my head. I said my shit all wrong. I didn't mean to make her upset. Fuck, that was the last thing I wanted to do. I was trying to sweep the shit under the rug so we both could go back to normal. I didn't think, for one second, it would go down like that.

Due to my lack of sleep, I'm off my game, so I ask the Prez if I could trade places with ZZ, and stay here on watch. With my head clouded and confused, there is no way I will be able to focus in that meeting with the Chinese. I might miss the smallest movements, and in doing so, cost one of my brothers their life if that shit goes down the wrong way.

When he agrees, I'm thankful I am able to hang back with the others. We don't speak as our ladies rumble between our legs. We wait patiently while the others are inside.

After a few minutes, I'm confident I made the right call because all my focus circles right back to the conversation with Tatiana. It screeches in my mind like the needle on a broken vinyl record. Each way it plays reminds me how bad I fucked up that shit. There is no doubt in my mind that it will take an endless amount of time for her to forgive me. End being the key word, because I believe that she'll never forgive me for this. I think about what a life without her friendship will be like, and all I come up with is empty, blank, and meaningless. Those three words don't sit well with me.

Fuck!

I'm empty enough. I have no desire to become a bottomless pit, and that is what will happen if I don't fix this as soon as possible. She's truly my only real friend. She may not know much, but she knows more than the others do, because she is the only person who can look through the black.

She can see past it.

The sound of roaring motorcycles brings me back from my thoughts. We all breathe a long sigh. I don't think anyone was ready to turn things red today. The brothers are sick and tired of bloodshed. We've had enough of it to last two lifetimes.

But when the Prez roars past us, nodding in the direction of home, he looks none-too-pleased with the outcome of the situation. As soon as they've all sped by, the rest of us pull out right behind them.

***

Once we park our bikes, we head straight to church. Sitting around the table, we wait patiently for our Prez, and when he enters the room, he slams the door, walks over to his chair, and kicks it so hard that it shatters once it hits the wall. We wait for him to calm. No one dares to speak. No one dares to make a sound. Hell, no one dares to make a move.

"Fuck," he roars while fisting his hair. His face turns red with rip-roaring anger. "That motherfucker."

Jesus Christ, it must have been bad, worse than what half of us think.

"I can't believe I let her talk me into this fuckin' shit." His loud voice booms throughout the room.

Oh shit… he's pissed, at not only the Chinese, but also his wife. I have no doubt that each one of us is thinking the same fucking thing. The club is going to be tense for a little while. When mom and dad can't play nice, the kids aren't happy.

"Her little control issue cost me 11.5 million fucking dollars. Goddamn, this is bullshit," he rants, his fist clenching and unclenching.

Cost him? It cost the damn club. We've earned that shit. A thermometer is not needed to feel how hot it is in this room. The smell of anger from the fuming bodies is so thick in the room, I can almost taste it on my tongue. The amount of money we're paying for this project has more than one of us blazing with rage.

"Never in my goddamn life have I bowed down like that." He tilts his head to the ceiling and howls in anger.

I grab my face in my hands, shaking my head in disbelief. Not only did we lose a truckload of money, our Prez looked weak. This truly is a hard hit on the club, and he has every right to be as angry as he is.

"I'll give you the fucking money, jackass," Winter screams through the closed door.

Oh god, Winter, really? This is club business. She is only going to make this worse than it is. What is she even doing listening in through the door? She knows better than that. All the women do.

"Don't you fucking start your shit with me, Angel. You haven't seen mad until you've seen me like this," Prez spits out as he paces back and forth.

The door splinters open, revealing a seething Winter holding a gun straight at our Prez. She kicked the door right open. Gunfire crackles through the air as the door splinters open. A furious Winter stalks in, her gun pointing straight at our Prez. Groans sound out around the table. The pregnancy hormones Prez constantly refers to are clearly controlling Winter's thinking.

"Everyone... get the fuck out. I demand to speak to my husband!"

None of us moves, and she fires off a round into the wall behind my head.

I lower myself in my chair.

Sniper curses as he jumps up from his chair and positions himself in front of our Prez. His Sergeant-at-Arms patch brings him smack dab in the middle of the couple's argument.

"Please, don't make me clip you in the knees, Winter. You're carrying my niece or nephew," Sniper pleads as his body covers the Prez. "You know, as soon as the sound of wood splitting echoed into this room, I've had this gun trained on you."

Prez peers over Sniper's shoulder with a look so cold, I'd be scared if I were Winter right now.

"Sniper... you threatening me? You've seen me shoot, and you know what the fuck I can do with this gun. Clip me, I fucking dare you. I may fall, but I'll be landing a bullet in your forehead as I drop to the floor. I'll let you think about that for a moment."

Fuck, this shit seriously hit a whole new level.

"Put one in her foot, Sniper," Prez growls from behind him.

He cannot be serious. That is his fucking pregnant wife!

All of a sudden, before anyone can blink, matters move in a whole different direction. Tatiana, Storm, and Piper rush into the room and surround Winter.

"This has gotten so far out of control. I'm ashamed to be a part of this family!" Tatiana yells. "Go ahead. Shoot through me, Uncle Sniper. You won't last long before there's a bullet in your head."

Sniper snarls at her and it only furthers the women's anger.

"What? You can threaten a pregnant woman with a bullet, but when a woman threatens you, you fucking growl? All of you need to get a fucking grip. You knew we were out there in the community room! You knew we could hear." Tatiana tilts her head up, blows out a steaming hot breath, and peers back at Prez. "You made it easy for us, Braxxon. You were roaring at the top of your lungs. You're all acting like a bunch of spoiled, roughed-up kids." She spits that last word out and I know it is directed at me, more than the others. "All of you, lower your fucking guns. Right now!"

No one moves.

"I said lower your damn guns," she orders. Her body shakes with anger, her face heats up, and her eyes narrow sternly.

Woah!

"Tatiana, darlin', I think it's best if you go back outside. Right. Now," ZZ says as he stands.

"Don't bother, Dad. I swear on all that is holy, I ain't leaving this room until every member of this family has lowered their guns." She snatches up the trashcan, turns it upside down, and empties the contents all over the floor. She then walks over to Sniper first. "Put your gun in here, right now." He doesn't move. "I said now, Uncle Sniper."

She taps her foot until he drops his gun into the trashcan. "This is why, back in the day, y'all had the no gun rule in church." The entire room sits in shock, including me. No one has seen this side of Tatiana. She is furious, demanding, and not at all acting as a child. You could hear a pin drop at the silence in the room when she is not speaking. She commands the room as if it is her own personal bitch. "Oh, stop looking at me like that. You've all had me trapped here too many times for me not to see EV-REE little thing." To stress her point, she nudges Sniper with the trashcan. "The one in your right boot, as well."

Sniper tilts his head to the side. "How in the fuck?"

"Again." Tatiana sighs. "You've trapped me here, oh, how many times? And Godfather, I want both of yours too, as well as your knife." She shakes the trashcan behind Sniper's back. "In fact, all of you, very slowly, take all your guns out and lay them on the table."

Again, no one moves, but me. She has a point. This shit has gotten so far out of control, there will be no coming back from it if she doesn't do this.

"Why aren't you taking Winter's gun," Prez grumbles as he puts his pieces and knife into the trash.

"Oh, I dunno, maybe because she's pregnant, and you ordered your brother to shoot her in the foot? By the way, you better watch yourself, or you might find that you're brushing your teeth with a dirty toothbrush." Tea's voice cracks with her words, her heart spilling out with each sentence. Sadness drips with each syllable. She raises her hand to swipe the tears streaming down her face. "I'll be damned if I'll lose another family member because you fucknuts are angry and taking it out on one another. You're lucky Grandma Berry is at her house with Mace right now. She'd shoot all of you for acting like this."

It takes a good five minutes for her to collect all the guns, and once she does a mental rundown in her head, she speaks again. "Winter, yours now." Tatiana holds the can out to her. "The other one, as well. Seriously? I know most of your deepest secrets, so stop trying to pull one over on me." Tatiana says, exasperated, one hand going to her hip in aggravation. "Dad, stop smirking. I know your brass knuckles are hidden behind your wallet, and so help me god, Rap, if you even think about reaching under your cushion for the knife that I call a sword, I will roll your ass off a cliff."

Once she is satisfied she has all the main weapons, she gets down to business.

"Winter, go nest somewhere," she orders. When Winter doesn't move, Tatiana snaps at her. "GO!"

"I'm going." Winter throws her hands in the air as she walks out of the room.

"You both need to go, as well." She glares at Piper and Storm. "I'm sorry, but I've been in this family for almost nineteen years, and it's time I start speaking up. If they want to share with you, they can, but for now, leave." She points to the door. "And shut what's left of that door behind you."

When the door closes behind the women, Tea sets the trashcan down and crosses her arms.

"Well, I can honestly say I have never once been ashamed of my family, until this moment. Yeah, sometimes it sucks being a part of it, but I have never, and I mean never, been so let down in all my life." Sadness drizzles from her tone.

"Here is how this is going to go. Braxxon, and yes, I called you Braxxon, not Godfather. You will have to earn that title back because you sure as hell don't deserve it right now. You can be pissed at your wife all you want, but you cannot, and I can't stress this enough, you cannot order your brother to shoot her! What in the hell were you thinking?" She stares at Braxxon, waiting for his response, but he lowers his gaze to the floor in shame, and doesn't speak.

"That's right. You're ashamed of yourself too, now, aren't ya? Well, you should be." She takes a deep breath before continuing. "You will let yourself cool down, and when you can rationally talk to your wife again, you may leave this room, and not a moment sooner than that. I'll be watching you."

She turns to Sniper and hits his shoulder. "And don't even get me started on you, Sniper. Yeah, you lost the uncle shit, too. You were actually going to shoot her! I have half a mind to tell Grandma Berry, so she can poison you for a month straight! You think Pop is proud, looking down on the lot of you right now?" A look of disgust covers her face. "He's probably looking down with pity and shame that his sons would even think about shooting a woman, let alone a woman carrying his grandchild!"

"Y'all may be grown ass men, but that shit that just happened," she gestures around the room, "is childish behavior, and since y'all want to act like children, I am going to treat y'all like that. Timeout until your shit is cooled."

Tatiana sighs now that she's finished chastising the adults for their wrong behavior. It is ironic how I kept calling her a child, and now, she is the only reasonable adult in the room. And fuck if she doesn't look stunning in my eyes.

"I am tired, so damn tired of the drama and the violence. I get that you're in an MC. I do. But don't ever turn your back on family again. This isn't how we function. Take all this hate and direct it towards the people who deserve it, not on the people who love you more than life itself." She shakes her head back and forth a few times before turning her attention to me.

Oh, shit. I didn't do anything!

"Shadow, if you want to get off my shit list, you can sit outside those doors and hand the guns back when people leave this room, calm—"

I don't even let her finish before my ass is out of the chair and over to the door, grabbing the trashcan filled with guns on my way. This is my easy out and I'm not stupid. My brain is screaming, "take the offer," before she even finishes issuing it.

She looks around the room one more time and shakes her head in disgust before opening the door to leave. When it shuts behind her, I swear I can hear crickets in the silence that lingers.

"Did we fucking get smacked down by my daughter," ZZ asks in disbelief, his voice echoing in the quiet room.

"The Chinese didn't even bust my balls like that," Prez says as he walks over and kicks the shattered pieces of his chair. "What in the fuck?"

They can talk all they want about what happened, but I will not be a part of it. I came dangerously close to ripping off my patch when this shit started. Shooting a woman? The Prez has a lot of respect to earn back from a few of us. I say nothing as I let myself out the door.

"Tatiana gave me strict orders, and she was in fucking tears when she went flying out of here." Piper looks up as she rolls a

72

chair over to me. "You guys fucked with her head so hard with that shit."

Pain slices through my chest as I try to imagine everything Tea has to be feeling. Not only did we get into it, but she also lashed out at her entire family. With good reason, of course, but shit, she has to be drained. "Go to her. Please, Piper. I won't move from this chair until everything is good. I swear to god."

Piper studies me and considers my answer before she gives me hers. "I'll go to her, but if even a drop of blood is spilled while I'm gone..."

I nod. She doesn't have to finish.

"Okay, Storm and Winter are cleaning out the office if anyone asks. Make sure they're calm enough, though, before you tell them where they are."

Again, I nod.

What a fucking day. I have not only spoken down to Tatiana by pure accident, but I have lost almost all the respect I had for my President. Today is one of those days I wish I could take back and do over, so I could stop to fix things before they escalate.

***

Chapter Nine

Shadow

After about two hours, I have given weapons back to everyone, so I step outside to get some fresh air. As I light up my smoke, I see items flying out of the office doorway. Winter's curses travel through the open window, and Storm leans against the building, shaking her head. I'm no pregnancy expert, but I am almost positive Winter shouldn't be lifting all that stuff. I mouth, "what the fuck," to Storm, and her head continues to shake back and forth in a "don't bother" manner.

"This place is a mess. How in the hell did they ever keep track of their work!" Winter huffs as she tosses an empty filing cabinet out of the office.

Everyone has finally cooled off, but if Prez sees her lifting and throwing office furniture, all hell will break loose. I groan, sidestepping the cast out items, and make my way to the door.

"Winter. I don't think you're supposed to be doing that. Prez would probably get pissed."

I duck as a folding chair soars above my head, narrowly missing me. "Christ! You could've knocked me out!"

Piper comes from across the courtyard, and when she sees the look on my face, she mouths that Tatiana is sleeping, and I nod a thank you as another item flies over my head. I point my finger towards the clubhouse, and Piper takes the hint that I want some help with this.

What the hell is going on with this damn club? This has to be the weirdest damn day of my life. Something has to be in the water. Everyone is losing it.

The bell on the gate rings. Winter and Storm ignore it, and I don't see a prospect in sight. This place is falling the fuck apart. If I wanted to play the part of a greeter, my ass would be working at a department store. Storm's cackles fill the air while I grumble and walk up to the gate.

I should have gone nomad, that's what I should have done, instead of coming to a place where the women secretly run this shit. The others might not see it, but I do. The women here have invisible crowns and snicker behind our backs every chance they get.

When I peer through the peephole, my head shakes at the ghost standing before me. This can't be right. This can't be. I look again, and my eyes do not deceive me. What in the—

I scramble to hit the switch for the gate to open, and then take a step back. When a woman with long, jet-black hair looks up from the envelope in her hand, my heart stops. All that comes to my mind is Lana…

Of all days for this to happen, it would be today. I gesture her in, and take her rollaway bag before shutting the gate.

"Hi, I'm—"

I shake my head. "I know who you look like, so I'm going to assume you're Lana's sister?"

"Yes, my name is Akela. This was my sister's last known address," she says quietly as she peers down at the envelope. "I haven't heard from her in months."

All of it starts to make sense because we never could locate Lana's cell phone after everything happened.

"May I?" I ask, and she hands over the envelope. I can't

believe what I am seeing. Lana wrote her sister from this address not long before she was killed. And Akela doesn't even know her sister is dead. Oh, fuck.

"Shadow, who was at the—," Winter's voice cuts off as she comes around the corner and gets her first look at Lana's sister. Tears fill her eyes as her trembling hand comes to her mouth. Winter shakes her head back and forth in disbelief. "I... I... I don't understand," she cries through her fingers. I step back as Winter walks up to this woman who could, for all intents and purposes, be Lana's twin. I don't want to even imagine how it will make Winter feel to tell this beautiful woman her sister has been dead for months. When Akela turns her body to face Winter, my biggest fear for this entire situation walks up fast behind me.

"Lana," he croaks.

I reach out to stop him, but my movements are too slow. He grabs her elbow and spins her around towards him. With his first full look at her, he steps back quickly, shocked to silence. His eyebrows pull together and pain spreads across his face as his eyes bounce over features that bear an uncanny resemblance to his beloved Lana.

"What is going...," Storm's interruption fades at the sight of Akela, and she stumbles backwards from shock.

"You guys, Braxxon wants to know who was the woman at the gate that he saw on the clubhouse mon–" Piper cuts herself off. "No, no way," she gasps.

As she takes in all the expressions, Akela squeaks a nervous laugh. She has no clue what the tears, looks of disbelief, and the mere shock of her presence means to the people around her. My gaze moves back to Pyro. His shades now cover his eyes, no doubt to hide his pain.

"Shadow… take Pyro into the club, uh, into the clubhouse for a drink," Winter orders in a pain laced tone. I don't argue with her. I can't. I won't. This is too much for everyone. I get that.

"You got it, First Lady." I place one arm around Pyro's shoulders and drag Akela's rollaway bag beside us.

"Wait!" Akela's voice stops us. "You're Pyro? You're my sister's lover?"

How in the fuck? My eyes drop to the letter as Pyro groans in agony. FUCK!

"Pyro, go," Winter pleads as tears pour from her eyes.

"C'mon, you don't want to be here for this, man. You don't," I say in a voice low enough that only he can hear.

"I… I… fuck, brother," he croaks.

I pat him hard on the back as we walk into the clubhouse. Our president looks pissed off until he gets a load of the agony laced across the almighty Pyro's face. "What the fuck happened?"

As I push Pyro towards a barstool, I tell him. "Lana had a sister and she's here."

I don't bother to say anything else. The Prez gets it. Hell, we all get it. This is going to fuck a lot of people up.

"Are you fucking serious?"

Pyro takes the shot I pour him, gulps it, and his hand quivers as he holds the glass up for another. As I fix him another, I answer my Prez. "As a heart attack."

Pyro takes the bottle from my hands, lifts it to his mouth, and gulps the whiskey. When it dribbles out the side of his mouth, he stops and wipes his face on his sleeve. "She looks like her," he hisses as he tilts his head back for more firewater.

"Your wife is telling her now…" I let the sentence drag, hoping Prez catches my meaning.

"Oh hell, she is going to be a mess."

The sound of glass hitting the bar echoes, drawing our attention to a fuming Pyro.

"You fuckin' think?" he growls as he reaches over the countertop for more whiskey.

Jesus, he's going to kill himself.

I look over at our Prez for an answer as to what the fuck we're supposed to do about this? He gives me no answer as he moves his attention to the monitor above the bar. My eyes follow. I crave pain but not this kind. This kind of pain is emotional and far more disturbing than the pain that I enjoy lashing out.

"I'm the biggest fuckin' prick there is," Prez groans while rubbing his temples.

I say nothing, because he doesn't want to hear what I have to say. In all honesty, I am so damn disappointed in this club, and we all have enough shit to deal with, without me saying Prez was in the wrong. I will let this one slide for now, even though I don't condone what he did.

The door to the clubhouse opens. Sniffles fill the air as the door shuts behind them. Winter, Storm, and Piper escort a distraught Akela towards the cabinet that holds all of the fallen. Pyro's head turns slowly, his eyes trailing her, watching, as if, at any moment, she'll magically become Lana. He turns back towards the bar and lifts the bottle to his lips.

Prez removes the keys chained at his side, walks to the cabinet, and unlocks it. The room goes silent when he takes Lana's remains out and hands them to Akela. Her sobs echo as she squeezes the urn tightly to her chest. Her entire body trembles as she mourns the loss of her sister. She shifts, cranes her neck, and looks at Pyro's back. Firming her grip on the last piece she will ever hold of her sister, she moves slowly, cautiously towards him, Lana's last words to her rustling against the urn. Tears streaming down her solemn face, she nudges herself onto a bar stool, sets Lana's ashes down, and slides the envelope towards Pyro. His light puffs of breath as he turns to face her are the only sounds filtering through the air.

"I don't...," she sniffles, "I don't know the extent of what you...," she clears her throat to gain control of her cracked voice, while wiping the salty diamonds cascading down her face, "of what you had with my sister, but I think you should read this."

Every eye in the room follows his shaky hand as it slides across the bar towards the envelope. He stops and pulls back a few times before finally resting his fingers on top of it.

Piper moves behind the bar, wets a rag, and hands it to Akela. Her 'thank you' is barely audible as she wipes the tears off her face. "You can keep that letter, Pyro. I...," she huffs out a sigh and wipes her cheeks again, "I think you're going to want to keep it." She takes a deep breath. "No, you should keep it."

The air is tense. No one moves. Hell, no one is even breathing right now as we wait for his response. They stare at one another before he slowly slides the envelope towards him. "Thank you," he croaks. "I'm so sorry for your loss."

She closes her eyes before she whispers, "You, too."

Pyro picks the letter up, stands, and after taking one last look at her, he moves towards the hall leading to the apartments.

"Piper, can you show Akela to a room, please?" Winter says, her voice choked with tears.

When Akela hears her name, the devastating look on her face strikes my heart. "Can I please stay where my sister was when she wrote me?"

We look back and forth at each other as we try to figure out where Lana would have been at the time she wrote the letter to her mystery sister. Since none of us has a clue, I hope that Akela knows.

"She called it…," she chuckles softly while wiping her nose, "she called it the slam room in her letter."

The room erupts in easy laughter as she smiles at all of us.

"You can stay anywhere you want to, darlin'," Prez says as he wraps Winter in his arms.

"Did you keep my sister's belongings? Her lei is needed. It's the light blue and pink one she wore at our parents' funeral," Akela asks, hope shining in her eyes.

Winter answers, "Yes, I know the one. I'll get it for you," and takes off down the hall and out of the clubhouse.

Akela stands. "I wish to say a prayer."

Why didn't we think to do this? Our faces read the same thing. We knew Lana was Hawaiian and her culture was significant to her. I think it was one of those things that attracted Pyro to her in the first place.

"It's more of a Hawaiian goodbye," she whispers in a quiet voice.

A few moments later, Winter returns with the bag that holds the lei. Akela takes it from her, opens it, and gently spreads the garland of dried flowers. After sliding the wreath of plumerias and orchids over her head, she picks up Lana's urn and turns to Winter. "Please, don't throw away that bag."

I take a closer look at the bag and see dried flowers and greenery inside of it.

Storm walks over to Akela and laces their arms together. "I'll take you to the roof of one of the buildings. You'll have your privacy."

Akela looks at her, smiles, and then thanks everyone for their kindness before they trail out of the building.

"Braxx, can you take me to our room so I can process all of this," Winter says quietly.

Prez says nothing as he guides her towards the exit, and as they walk out, I follow. My lungs lust for fresh air. Sadness has suffocated the inside of that room.

***

Chapter Ten

Shadow

Berry and Mace return while I'm outside smoking and watching Akela as she prepares for Lana's ceremony on top of the live-in building. They are walking towards me when Pyro comes out of the clubhouse and immediately hones in on Akela. As Berry gets closer, she looks to see what has caught Pyro's attention. Her loud gasp echoes around the courtyard when she sees Lana's look alike.

"Unbelievable," she whispers.

Mace must sense the importance of what is happening, because he says nothing, and the four of us appreciate the beauty of the entire ceremony. We can't hear the words she sings, but the melody rings clear in our ears. Akela continues her mournful song for a little while longer, and when she is finished, she opens the urn, tilts it, and lets the wind carry the ashes. Moments pass, but no one speaks as we watch Lana's remains floating free on the breeze. I look back towards my brother to see him lift his shades and swipe at his eyes before allowing them to once again cover his anguish and grief.

"That was beautiful. I assume she's a relative?"

With Berry's question, my attention snaps back to Lana's grieving sister. Her body slumped in a defeated stance, and her shoulders hiccupping with each breath in and out, is one of the saddest things I have ever witnessed. People assume pain like this isn't visible, but it is. One look at Akela and her pain is clearly written all over her.

I force my sight off Akela to look at Berry. "Her sister."

"Oh, dear," Berry whispers as her shaky hands grip the purse at her side. When she looks at me, her broken expression reveals the pain the club has felt and the pain Akela is experiencing. So much of our misery is stacked in her gaze that my chest burns.

"I only came by to drop Mace off…" she trails off as if she needs to offer an excuse.

When I don't say anything in return, her gaze seeks out Akela once again, a hiccup escaping her throat as she finds her.

Of all the things that have happened today, this one occasion has shocked us all to the core. Lana may have only been here for a short time, but she made an impact on the lives of everyone she touched. Even though I didn't know her well, the times we did talk let me know she was a genuine person with a kind heart. It was a tragic event, and most won't ever heal from it.

As Akela leaves the roof of the live-in, everything stops while we wait for her to enter the courtyard. Moments later, she comes out the door, looks around, and once her eyes land on him, she heads straight for Pyro. Her movements are delicate and beautiful for someone feeling so much pain. When she stops in front of him, she places one hand on his cheek and hands him the urn while speaking to him in a gentle, soothing voice. Even though her words are too quiet for us to hear, we can see their faces, and his expression contorts into the purest agony I have ever seen in my life. She brings her hand down, and he gestures for her to follow him. He must be showing her the slam room, or they might be going somewhere to talk. I hope that everyone leaves them alone. Pyro needs this time with someone from Lana's family in order to gain some sort of peace from losing her.

"Without getting into their business, can someone please tell me a little of what just happened?"

Shit. Poor Mace. I completely forgot he wasn't even here when all this went down. The look on his face is one of pure confusion, so I dig out a smoke, light it, and explain. "You've heard us talk about the run-in with the Russians, and the people who were murdered, right? And the woman that Pyro was, or rather, still is in love with, was one of them." I tug my hair as the image of Akela releasing Lana's ashes plays through my mind. "Well, that's Lana's sister, Akela. We had no fucking clue there was a sister, so when she came to the gate with this fucking letter that Lana wrote, it fucking rocked the club. She didn't even know Lana was dead. Man, this shit is fucked up," I convey with lungs full of smoke.

Mace nods his head, understanding the awkwardness a little better.

"I think I will grill a big dinner for the family tonight. Mace, will you help me?" Berry interrupts us, and Mace smiles at his grandmother, wraps his arm around her shoulder, and tells her to lead the way.

My shoulders slump forward as the events of the day wear on my body. I trudge across the compound parking lot and into the live-in building. Each step up the stairs feels like ten as I climb the stairs to the floor where my room is. Once I reach my door and unlock it, I walk in and flop face down on my bed. The soft, pillow top mattress soothes my aching body upon impact, and I groan in relief. When my sunglasses dig into my face, I lift my head enough to tear them off and toss them on my nightstand. As my head hits the bed again, I notice my door standing wide open, which is unlike me. I like my privacy and it wins out, so I drag myself back up to close it. Once it clicks shut, I kick off my boots and shrug out of my cut. My shirt follows and my jeans last. I flip the switch that turns on my ceiling fan. I move to my bed and sit on the edge while I burrow my face into my hands and rub them back and forth to lessen some of the tension from my pounding migraine.

After it subsides enough for me to lay down, I flop back and sink down onto my comforter, close my eyes, and drift off to sleep, vowing not to wake until the following day.

***

Chapter Eleven

Tatiana

When I wake to the smell of bacon, I look over at my clock and realize I have slept for fourteen hours. That showdown must have done a number on me if I was asleep that long. I throw back my sheet, sit up, and reach for the clip attached to the post of my bed. I twist my hair and pin it up out of my face while I walk towards the bathroom to brush my teeth.

When I finish scrubbing them clean, I swish a little mouthwash, spit it out, and let the water rinse it down the drain. I stare at my reflection in the mirror. Although it looks as if I'm well rested, it doesn't feel that way to me. My eyes look bluer, my skin appears clearer, but peering into my own soul, I know my reflection is a false image.

I toe on my slippers and walk downstairs towards the aroma that woke me. With all the noise I hear, I know that my grandma Berry is cooking breakfast for the entire family before I'm even in view of the cluttered tables.

"There's the sleepyhead," Grandma Berry chirps. "You missed one heck of a dinner last night, kiddo."

I stretch, and when I go to sit, my eyes deceive me. I do a double take, turn, and look at Winter before she motions for me to lean down to her.

"It's Lana's sister. She knows what happened, and we're welcoming her," she whispers. "So, wipe that surprised look off your face."

I take my seat as my grandma hands me a plate stacked high with eggs, bacon, sausage, and toast. My stomach growls with joy at the amount of food on my plate. Sleeping that long has really unbalanced me, but as I dig into my food, my eyes wander back to the beautiful Lana look alike. It's strange but also calming. It almost feels as if she's back here with us.

When Shadow takes his plate to the sink and kisses my grandma on the forehead to thank her for a delicious breakfast, my heart pitter-patters. He can be so sweet at times and yet, such a dick too, but when I see him interacting with my grandmother like this, it makes the feelings I've developed that much stronger. Shadow makes me weak without him even realizing he's doing it. He holds so much power over me, and no matter how angry I am at him, he still makes me tremble in the knees every single time I lay eyes on him. It is the most aggravating thing I have ever felt.

"You guys… I'm taking a wild guess here, but based on my sister's letter, I'm assuming this extra quiet behavior is unusual." Akela laughs nervously as she draws my attention from Shadow.

The bacon stops midway to my mouth at her statement. It is a bold one, that is certain, but it is also a true statement.

"We're letting the guys practice hospitality."

I laugh out loud at Winter, and the rest of the room follows.

"Would you guys like to hear a story about her?" She takes a deep breath. "It's one of my favorites."

When she asks that, Pyro tenses up. With a sad smile, I look over at my uncle. To know he lost her, right around the same time he fell in love with her, is enough to make me weep for him.

"I'd like to hear it," he mumbles after a few quiet moments.

Akela places her orange juice down on the table and inhales deeply again before taking us on a Lana filled journey.

"The sun was shining so bright this day. You couldn't even look up and see the beautiful clouds in the sky, because when you tried, the sun's beams would blind you. Lana was about fifteen or so. My parents were rather strict when it came to letting Lana go to the beach. She was four, almost five years younger than me. So whenever she wanted to go, she would call me up." Akela's lips tilt up to form a smile as she laughs at the memory.

"This day was different than our other trips. Something about the atmosphere, I guess, or maybe because it was one of the many surf seasons, and the beach was extra packed, but whatever. Something made me watch her like a hawk. It felt completely off." She stops, picks up her glass of orange juice, takes a sip to wet her throat, and then sets it back down on the table.

"Not even an hour after we got there, all hell broke loose. Sharks had invaded the surf. There must have been at least a dozen of them. With all the people in the water, it drew so much attention to the surfers who were out in the deep, waiting to catch some waves." Her head shakes back and forth like she still can't believe it. "My stomach was in knots. I paced this little patch of sand back and forth, trying to keep track of her in the crystal blue waters. Every single time I would spot her, she would disappear again. It was nerve racking. When one of the sharks attacked—" she cuts herself off and then starts again, "well crap, this isn't a story to share while people are eating. I apologize."

Smiles light up the room as Godfather speaks. "You do realize you're in an MC, right? Go on, darlin'. You aren't offending anyone."

She smiles back and nods at him. "The first attack happened so fast. I decided to swim out to find Lana, because the screams were so loud, there's no way she could hear me calling for her. My body was shaking, and I was panicking so bad that I'm surprised I didn't drown myself. When I finally laid eyes on her, she was paddling this guy in on his surfboard. That's when my heart stopped, right then and there." Her hand flies to her heart, and her fingernails dig into her shirt as if she can still feel the pain in her chest.

"This guy's leg was gone below the knee. It had been bitten off by one of the sharks. The water around them was filled with blood. It was so thick, all I could think was the next attack would be on my sister. By the time I reached them, she was screaming for me to paddle him in, and right beside us, a shark attacked another surfer who was trying to catch a wave to get to shore. She pushed the guy on the surfboard to me and yelled for me to get him help, and then she swam back out," she says while wrapping her arms around her chest to comfort herself. I'm surprised she is still speaking, let alone telling a story of her sister. The memory has to hurt.

"My fifteen-year-old sister was risking her own damn life for complete strangers. I couldn't dwell on that, at the time. Later on, I would be proud of her, but at that moment, I was anything but. It is amazing what you feel when your own flesh and blood puts themselves in harm's way for complete strangers. I was so damn angry, and I'm not proud of the fact that I wanted to leave the guy to fend for his own life, so I could drag my sister to shore." She shakes her head back and forth as if she is completely disgusted with herself over the thought.

"I finally broke through all the bodies to get this guy onto the beach, and the lifeguards took over while I started searching the water for my sister again. This time, I got the scare of my life. When I finally found her helping another surfer, I saw a fin swimming around them. At first, I couldn't tell if the guy was missing a limb, but I could see he was gushing blood everywhere, and as the shark moved around them, its circle got smaller and smaller. It felt like someone had taken that one moment out of a movie and inserted it into my real life." Her body shudders. "You hear people say they were frozen in one spot. Well, I was rooted to the sand. I couldn't move. I couldn't breathe. I couldn't scream. All I could do was stand there in shock, scared for my sister's life." Her arms move from around her body, and one hand swipes at the lone tear escaping her left eye.

"She didn't let that fin deter her, not one little bit. She kept on kicking that surfer in as that shark circled. Every time it was to her side and then behind her, she would kick. When it was in front of her, she would stop and watch, waiting for it to pass before kicking again. It was like she was playing a game with it. A game of smarts, if you will, and it was almost as if the shark was trying to figure her out. To this day, it was the most terrifying experience I have ever had. It continued back and forth like that until she was on shore. Someone even videoed it. You can probably still find it online. Anyways, she got him up to the sand and collapsed to catch her breath. She was covered in blood from head to toe, and the paramedics checked her body to make sure she wasn't injured." She stops and looks around at everyone.

"I guess the point that I'm trying to make with this story is this. Even then, she risked her life for others, and when Winter told me what probably went down when she died, it doesn't shock me in the least. Lana has always been the self-sacrificing type, and she went down exactly how she was supposed to. Defending others, because she always said, "What makes their life more important than mine?" Even though I'm so heartbroken she isn't here anymore, I know there wasn't a better way for her to be taken from me, from us. She went out

90

in a selfless battle, defending the people she cared about."

Tears cascade down my face when she stops talking. I think I understand Lana a lot better from hearing this one story, and my heart hurts knowing she was always that selfless. That kind. That real.

"Thank you, Akela." Pyro stands and leaves the room without even bothering to put his plate in the sink. That is how I know Akela's story hurt him very deeply. No one ever fails to clean up after themselves when my grandmother cooks. I grab his plate and take it over to the sink with mine, before slipping back upstairs and crying like the human her story reminded me that I was.

***

Chapter Twelve

Shadow

This morning at breakfast was the first time I've ever seen my brothers quiet all at once. The story Lana's sister told was life changing. It made me think I should never take life for granted, and others are as important as I am. I've never been that big of an asshole, but I can honestly say, I wouldn't have taken a bullet for someone I care about, much less a stranger. If Lana could swim in shark infested waters and risk her life to save a stranger's, why the hell can't I take a bullet for a loved one or maybe a woman or child?

Even though she's gone, her legacy affects those of us still here, and that means she lives on in us. It's made me realize I haven't done one single thing to fucking make my presence in the world worth anything yet. Do I deserve to be breathing, and do I take life for granted?

I scrub my face as I wait for our Prez to smack the gavel down. I'm sure he's going to tell me that it's time to set a meeting with Alec now that the Chinese are dealt with.

"Y'all know why we're here." He sits and smacks the gavel down on the table. "Now, let's get this shit over with. My wife is a fuckin' mess from that story earlier."

Pyro makes a sound that isn't quite human.

Fuck!

"Shadow, here is how I want this to play out. Go to your dude's club, do your thing, and act natural. When you're finished with your routine, be all casual and shit, and say my Prez wants a meetin' with you. If he asks why, shrug your shoulders," Prez orders.

"Easy enough."

"Set the meeting for the day after tomorrow, at two, at Club Sated. It won't be open, so we'll have control over everything, without bringing it back here to the compound." He adds.

"Done."

Prez looks down and then back up at us. "Winter is talkin' with Akela. She isn't to leave this compound without at least two patched members or two prospects. She's asked me if she could stay awhile. What the fuck was I supposed to say? No? We delivered a hard blow to her, and I ain't that fuckin' cold."

No one questions his decision to let her stay here. Why would we? He's the Prez. This is our club, but it is his club.

"Patch up, because my gut tells me we've had way too easy of a ride lately. Meetin' adjourned." The gavel smacks down hard against the wooden plank.

I hate how his last line replays over and over again in my head. More drama, more shit. Sometimes I wonder if this life is worth all of the crap we have to do so we can wear this fucking patch.

***

When I get to Euphoria, I stand along the wall and case my

surroundings, looking at Alec's every move. This isn't outside of my normal behavior. He calls it paranoia, but really, it's me paying attention. Everyone should pay fucking attention. If they did, half the shit that happens to them, wouldn't.

My head stays in one spot, and behind my shades, my eyes follow the people that I need to watch. They have no idea they're under surveillance. The color of my eyes isn't the only reason I wear dark glasses day and night. My friend's movements seem more off than usual, and tell me he is hiding something. That peaks my interest a whole lot. This, I remind myself, is why the Prez let me trade up and join the Master Charter, instead of going nomad. I'm proud to know the art of stalking, and I do very well at it.

Alec watches me more than normal, too. He keeps peeking over his shoulder to see if I'm where I was when he last looked, but he doesn't know I'm watching him as he does this. My back tenses when I get a sudden feeling of betrayal racing through my instincts.

What in the fuck did this fucker do? Does he know what we are planning to do?

All of this factors into how I handle telling him he has a meeting with my Prez tomorrow afternoon. I decide it's time I make my rounds, find someone to fuck and hurt, and satisfy that craving before I blow him away with my sudden news. I can't text my Prez to let him know something is off because I never take my phone out here. If I did, Alec would suspect me more. I do as the Prez says and just be myself.

I hunt down a little masochist with short brown hair that I've fucked in the past. It'll be quick and to the point, without any of the usual spiel. When I seek her out, she is chatting with one of her friends, waiting to see if I choose her.

94

I bend down and murmur in her ear. "Feather." I fucking hate that scene name, yet I respect her enough to use the weird fucker.

"Tavis," she answers in greeting.

"Come," I order.

I don't give her an option. She has never denied me, and if she wanted to, she would not have greeted me back. Great thing about repeaters, no pleasantries are needed.

Once my room door shuts behind us, she strips. God, I fucking love when I use repeaters I actually enjoy being with. They already know what's up, and I can get straight to the fucking and the pain.

"Color," I ask. This will be the only question since we know each other's scene limits. If she wants to inform me of something that has changed, she will, or she can safe word.

"Red as always," she responds as the dress slides off her curvy body. This is what I enjoy most about fucking Feather. She has curves, eats well, exercises, and watches over herself. She is one example of a perfect scene mate.

"And…"

Her lips tilt up and her Monroe piercing smiles at me. "I'm ready."

I toss my shades off, hang up my cut, and strip down before digging a condom out of my dresser and slipping it on. I don't like messing with them when I'm heated, and I don't like wasting time. I never pass up a quick scene with a repeater. It's too damn simple to please my demons.

I get my single tail out, and because I never use the same cracker, I attach a new one. I don't use it often, but it is not safe to use the same one on different scene mates because of the exchange of bodily fluids. When I crack it, the sound echoes the room and sings to me. The whoosh makes my balls tingle with the anticipation of splitting open her skin. Feather enjoys the pain. Hell, she begs for more. I only crack her on the back in one area, and never so hard that the lacerations won't easily heal.

"Your demons can come play whenever you're ready, Tavis," she purrs as she turns around and latches her hands into the braided rope hanging from the hooks in the ceiling.

"I'll strike you seven times, and no more," I growl.

Once I'm confident she is comfortable enough to let me strike her, I flick my single tail a few times to warm up my wrist. Feather's shoulder blades tense and loosen with each sound of the cracker. I line my eyesight up with the area we have agreed upon. I crack one more time, and then my wrists snaps, letting the leather whish through the air before the cracker swipes her skin. The sound of it slicing at her back makes my cock twitch and harden a little more. I flick again, and this time the skin tears enough to let out a trickle of blood. Her whimpers are of pleasurable pain, a sound I have come to love from her. By the time I'm on number six, blood trickles from all strikes and Feather now moans uncontrollably. The seventh one hits the hardest, and the sound of splitting skin is my undoing. I drop the whip to the floor and stalk towards Feather and as I wrap one arm around her body, I yank her towards me. Her back presses against my front as I put pressure against her wounds. With my free hand, I adjust the condom on my hard cock, and confident of its placing, I slip into her from behind and grip her tighter.

She cries out in pain, not pleasure, when her back scrubs against my front as I thrust into her repeatedly. My movements are strong and fierce, and the walls of her pussy clamp down and squeeze my cock.

When her hands release the ropes and her arms drop, I know my time with her is almost up and my release has to happen right now. I wet my thumb before I bring it to her ass and jam in it with enough force to make her bleed. Both holes being brutality pounded and her screams are all I need to free myself. I roar loudly as my cum spurts into the rubber.

I talk her down until she is comfortable enough for me to let go of her long enough to slip off my condom and get what I need to tend to her.

When the condom is tied, I drop it to the floor so that I can dispose of it later. I walk to the dresser, open my aftercare drawer, and grab the balm I will use on her wounds. I crave causing pain for sexual pleasure, but I always pay extra attention to the ones I harm, too.

"You want balm and wrap, Feather?"

She whimpers for both, so I grab some cloth before I walk back over to her. I lift her into my arms and carry her over to my bed and lay her flat on her stomach. I open the salve and dip my fingers into the palm and apply it to her skin. I do this until all seven lacerations are covered in cream. I then unroll the cloth and have her sit up straight. The ointment already doing its job of numbing her. Once the wrap completely covers her back, I help her slip back into her dress and kiss her on the forehead.

"Am I still needed?" I ask as I get dressed.

"As always, you've hurt me, fucked me, and then took great care in fixing me right up." Feather grins at me as she answers.

I nod as she lets herself out of my room.

Once I clean everything, I lock my room and head towards

Alec to deliver the blowing message that will make him see red. I locate him near the bar, and so no one can pick up on anything, I keep my back to the room. The conversation will be tense enough, and I'm afraid if he angers me, others would read it in my black eyes. I should have worn my fucking blue contacts. This is why I should always wear them, or at least keep them on me.

"Alec," I greet as nicely as I can. "My Prez wants a meetin' with ya the day after tomorrow."

"Is that so?" He sets his glass down and turns to give me his full attention.

"It is. The day after tomorrow, two o'clock at Club Sated." I roll my eyes.

He says nothing for a few seconds, and my patience with him begins to thin. It doesn't help that he has been letting certain things go when it comes to this club.

"I'll be there," he hisses as he picks up his glass.

That was too easy, and now I can't imagine what the fuck he has up his sleeve. I wonder what in the hell he might have heard, because he took that way too easily.

I head outside to my lady, throttle her on, and head to the club.

***

Back at the compound, I look for my Prez to let him in on the information about Alec. I find him playing a game of pool with Akela, Winter, and Sniper.

She sure looks like she's comfortable here.

"It's a little strange, isn't it?" Pyro says as he walks up to stand next to me.

Not to me, but I could see why he would say so.

The Prez spots me, hands his pool stick off to Winter, and strides towards me.

"And…"

I cross my arms, peer behind him, and notice we have the attention on us, so I say what I have to as quietly as possible without leading us away.

"It went how we expected, and I spot grey."

He scowls when I say grey. Grey means shady in our world. He isn't happy, and he shouldn't be. Who knows what the fuck is going to happen because of this shit.

"Thanks, brother."

I nod as he turns and walks back over to his game.

"Well, ain't that shit. I was hoping she'd get to leave here unscathed," Pyro hisses under his breath.

I know his comment is about Akela. She has been damaged enough by the news delivered to her when she arrived. Everything seems to go awry when new women appear. It is like their beauty beckons hell to rain down on us.

"I know," I respond.

But once the Prez says something, he sticks to it. He's already told her she could stay, and he isn't about to revoke that. I think it's more for Pyro's benefit than Akela's.

"Here we fuckin' go again," he growls more so under his breath than out loud.

I close my eyes as exhaustion takes over. "I'm hittin' the sack, brother."

He smacks me on the shoulder as I make my way towards the live-in.

***

Chapter Thirteen

Tatiana

I can't even go to the gas station by myself. It seems like every other month, I'm on lockdown or require an escort to leave the compound.

Even though I have my room in the live-in building, I still miss the feel of my own bedroom and childhood belongings that are in my dad's house off the compound. I honestly can't remember the last time I was actually there longer than an hour to pick up something. Grandma goes a few times a week to dust, sweep, and mop, and I constantly tell her it's a waste of her time to do those things. We're never there anyways. Her response is always the same. Every child needs a place to call home, and that home should always be welcoming.

I gave up on trying telling her what to do a long time ago. It is no use. She does what she wants, when she wants, and how she wants. She is the epitome of old-fashioned when it comes to family and homes.

Now that Akela is at the compound, things seem off. I can't explain it, but it is like everyone is on pins and needles every second of the day. Add in the stress of the upcoming Euphoria takeover, and it fuels an already lit fire.

I don't mind her being here for one reason only.

In her own way, she is helping my Uncle Pyro heal by sharing stories of Lana's childhood and reminding him that Lana had truly loved him. Otherwise, she wouldn't have felt the need to write her sister all about Pyro right before her passing.

To top all of that off, the two jokesters in the family, acting a little strange towards one another, makes it even weirder around the compound. I don't know what Uncle Sniper and Piper's problem is, but someone needs to smack them. They almost remind me of Shadow and me. The attraction is there, visible for everyone to see, but neither one will move on it.

Well, okay, it is half of what Shadow and I act like. I know I want him, and I would act on it in a heartbeat. He is the one that is scared of moving towards me in any way that isn't friendship. It irritates me to no end, because even though I have told him we're fine again, deep down, we really aren't. I find myself wanting to talk to him a lot less than I used to. I still watch him, but not as closely as I used to. It all seems to be pointless to me. A girl can only daydream about a guy for so long before she decides to move on, and my wanting to do that grows stronger and stronger every day.

"Earth to Tatiana, do you want me to get out and pump the gas for you, darlin'?"

I scowl at Smokey before I open my car door. I hate when he escorts me places. He used to say nothing, but now he talks all the time, and no one can seem to shut him the hell up. I miss the quiet, mysterious side of him. This part of him always manages to piss me off. I slam my car door shut because I want him to know I'm angry he's my babysitter again. I have asked Godfather to give me someone else. Hell, I would even take dealing with my attraction to Shadow and have him escort me around instead of Smokey.

"Tatiana?"

I groan out loud at the sound of that voice. I turn towards him. Haden. My first love and the first guy to break my heart is right there getting gas on the other side of the pump. My luck, but why isn't he off at school?

"Haden? Hey, why aren't you at college right now?"

I don't bother with niceties. He lost that right when he cheated on me. He looks like hell, now that I look more closely at him. What the hell happened to him?

"Ugh, about that… I had to take a semester off. My mom passed away."

Shit. You and your fucking mouth, Tatiana.

"I'm sorry for your loss. Really, Haden, I'm truly sorry. Your mom was a great woman."

I wonder how I missed that in the obituaries. All of a sudden, I'm angry at myself because I had a great relationship with his mother when Haden and I were together.

He nods. "She was. Cancer is a bitch."

I agree, but she was perfectly healthy half a year ago. Haden must sense my confusion because he answers me like he's in my head.

"They found it too late." He sighs sadly.

This might seem trivial to ask him after he told me the news about his mom, but I need to know because this was a part of his life. He lived for this. "What about football?"

The look that comes over him breaks my damn heart in half.

"I had to give it up. Dad can't handle everything by himself. I can try out again when I go back, but I lost my full ride."

"That sucks, Haden. I feel like I need to keep apologizing." I stick my credit card into the pump and insert the nozzle into my car.

Haden pulls his cellphone out of his pocket then looks back at me. "Want to go and get some breakfast at Ma and Pop's, to catch up, for old time's sake?"

His question stuns me. We didn't end things on good terms, and here we both are being civil adults. My dad would be proud of how I am acting right now. I'll have to tell him I was around Haden without throwing a bitch fit later. "Sure, but the club is on lockdown again so I have an escort." I jam my thumb behind me, gesturing towards a bored Smokey. "I'll make him sit at a different table." I laugh.

"I've missed that laugh, Tatiana. It was always such a carefree sound."

I gulp. This isn't a Haden I recognize. He never once complimented or flattered me in any way, other than an occasional you look hot comment. My cheeks flush, and I whisper thank you. I mean, what else am I supposed to say? I used to be in love with this guy.

"Well... meet you at Ma and Pop's in ten?" I try to move the conversation into a different direction.

"Yeah, ten." He smiles.

Shit. I have never once seen a smile like that from him either. When I finish pumping my gas, I hang up the nozzle, tear my receipt from the slot, and get in my car. I take a deep breath, buckle my seatbelt, and start the engine.

"Was that Haden?"

Oh dammit, Smokey! Stop talking again. You were funner to hang out with then.

"It was," I say aggravated as I pull out of the parking lot and make my way to the restaurant.

"Hey, where are we going? We're only supposed to be getting

gas."

I wish I had some duct tape to shut him up!

"We're having breakfast with Haden, and your ass is sitting at your own table. You guys give me no damn privacy."

"One, I didn't wanna sit with your grumpy ass either, and two, this is gonna piss Shadow off. You know he worries about you." Smokey scowls at me.

What in the hell? Since when? That asshole doesn't worry about me. He is always fending himself off me. Guys truly do not understand the female sex. I'm glad I took Piper's advice to move on from Shadow. She was right to say I was wasting my time by going after him. I tried to argue with her about it for a few minutes, but then she said that not everyone will give in to temptation and their feelings. When she said that, it made me realize how much of my time and life I was wasting, waiting for Shadow to smart up about the two of us getting together.

Haden's being back home under tragic circumstances might be my saving grace from Shadow, if I start to hang out with Haden while he's home for the semester. It would give me a distraction and something to think about other than Shadow. The day I can go without thinking of him once will be the day I know I can truly live my life without ever having something to do with him other than friendship. I hope being friends with Haden and my plan to use this time with him at home will provide me with that one day that I need.

When we get to Ma and Pop's, I motion for Smokey to find another table, but before I can finish my sentence, I see Shadow eating breakfast and drinking coffee like it is an everyday thing. This isn't his routine, so what the hell is he doing here?

"On second thought, there's Shadow. Go sit with his ass."

Haden strolls in as soon as I take a seat in a window booth, far away from the guys. I want as much space between us as I can get.

"Look at that. You got double the protection, now," he teases as he takes a seat.

Wow! I love this Haden. It's sad his mom had to pass away for him to become the person in front of me. My heart aches at the thought that maybe he is trying to mask his pain this way.

"Right! You'd think I was of royal blood or something." I smile.

Haden takes it upon himself to order our old usual breakfast, and the memories that flood into my mind from our past make me want to cry. God, I really loved him, but when I caught him cheating on me, it demolished that feeling very quickly.

"So, what have you been up to? Did you not go to nursing school at all?"

Oh shit, I forgot he didn't know. "Nope. I'm doing online business management courses because, let's face it, I'd be failing all of my courses if I weren't doing something online. We go on lockdown way too much, and dad would worry if I lived on a campus. Even though he still acts pissed when people talk about my sudden change of mind."

He seems to understand my reasoning because he drops it. This is what I miss the most about the relationship we had. He always understood the lockdown process. He hated it, and he always voiced that he did, and ultimately, it is what ruined the bond we had. When a person is neglected, he or she will seek to find that connection with someone else. I don't give a shit if I am young, and have exactly one relationship under my belt. I know that people crave closeness with another person. It is the main reason my dad gave in and fell in love with Storm. She strayed from their friendship because she was in love with him, and it hurting her to be friends. When she started to back away slowly, my dad freaked. He craved, desired, and needed that bond with her, whether he wanted it or not. His heart failed at closing off towards her. She won, hands down, and the saying, all's fair in love and war is true. He battled long and hard before surrendering to her.

"It's really good to be talking with you again," he mumbles quietly as our food is placed on the table.

"It honestly is, isn't it?" I respond and then tell the waitress thank you.

"I see Shadow's feelings about me haven't changed," he teases as he forks at his pancakes.

I groan and twist my body to look. The scowl on his face forces a laugh to bubble from my throat. He has no reason to be looking at Haden like that. What happened between Haden and me is in the past. I quit dwelling on things months ago. Being friends with Piper is amazing because she teaches you how to enjoy life the best you can no matter what and she does it without even knowing she is doing it. She helps the family loosen up all the time.

"I've changed a lot over the past six months," I say as I take a bite of my pancakes.

His blue eyes search mine to see if I am telling the truth. He was always good at reading me.

"I don't think you've changed, babe. I think you're growing up, learning yourself."

See. He's so perceptive when it comes to me, and my heart squeezes when he calls me babe. The little butthead still has an effect on me. Who knew?

"It's good to talk with you, Haden. I hate that it had to happen under these circumstances though."

He takes a drink of his orange juice, sets it down, and wipes his mouth before speaking again.

"I know. God, we were together a long time, weren't we?"

"Since sixth grade. Wow, that's like what," I count in my head, "shit, six or so years. Seven school years we were together."

I hadn't realized it had been that long until now. Our relationship was there, and our friendship was the glue that probably held us together that long. In a way, he will always be my best friend. He may have broken my heart, but if I ever need him, deep down I have always known that he will be there for me. I guess it has taken a lot of maturing to realize that. I still have a lot more growing to do, but at least I can see everything for what it was now.

"Tatiana, believe me when I say, I'm truly sorry for messing it all up. I was selfish. I broke the trust you had in me and I'll forever regret that."

My hand slides across the table and laces with one of his. "I'd like us to be friends again, Haden. I really would. You're the only one from my childhood that understands my life, and I miss having someone to talk to about it. I know that's selfish of me, but in a way, I need someone on the outside that understands it all. Someone besides my family."

His thumb rubs against the back of my hand, and that single movement reminds me of the comfort I have always felt with him.

"No, I get it. In a way, you're the only one that really knows me too. We're tragic." He laughs lightheartedly.

"We are." I chuckle.

We banter back and forth while we eat, and when it's time to say goodbye, we promise to hang out more before he goes back to school. It feels good to have him back in my life. It's almost like he's a safety net for my feelings. He was always a good ear for when I needed an outlet. The end of our relationship was when everything went so darn sour between us.

I ignore the glares from Shadow when Smokey follows me to my car. The time spent with Haden was enough to make me forget all about him. Knowing this makes me sad, but relieved, at the same time. I had been building such a great friendship with Shadow and my feelings got in the way of that. It saddens me to realize that, with the right company, I can forget he exists, at least for a little while, but in all reality, I know it is necessary for me to move on.

I'm not ready to go back to the compound yet, so I tell Smokey he has to go to the mall with me. I need space, and the club is not a place I can get much of that. He's not happy with another detour, but he really doesn't have a say in the matter. As long as I have him as my escort, I can stay out late and do what I want. He'll get over it.

***

Chapter Fourteen

Shadow

(Part One)

I pace back and forth in frustration, anger, and horniness. What the fuck am I doing on the floor where her room is? Why? Why the fuck am I here? I can think of only one reason. I want her. I want her very badly.

Seeing her with that asshole at Ma and Pop's, where I had escaped to enjoy my motherfucking coffee and egg sandwich, lit my ass on fire. It fueled me with an anger I didn't realize existed inside of me. The demons clawed to get out, begging me to release them so they could unleash my pent up wrath on that little bastard. What was she thinking? That fucker cheated on her repeatedly. Fuck, who knows how many times and she could talk with him as if nothing ever happened? She could eat fucking breakfast with the little prick?

A growl escapes my lips as my pacing increases, and the anger boils the blood beneath my skin. And that hug? I thought I would come unglued, watching them embrace like that. I've honestly never been more pissed off in my life.

Could this be deeper? Could I actually want more than friendship with her? I shake my head as I stalk back and forth through the hall. That can't be it. She couldn't handle the demons lurking inside of me. I would not only ruin her. I would destroy her, and all the good that lies beneath her light blue eyes.

"Shadow?"

Jesus, fuck! I didn't even hear her come up. She has me so far off of my fucking game, it is unreal. They call me Shadow for a fucking reason. This sneaky bullshit is my job.

"Shadow," she repeats in frustration.

FUCK!

I grab her arm and drag her to her door. "Open it," I growl.

I'm acting like a fucking animal right now. This isn't me. Everything I do is about self control. I'm in charge of things that deal directly with me.

"Shadow… you're acting weird."

I jerk the key from her hand, slide it in the lock, and turn. After the tumbler clicks, I pull it out, push open the door, and shove her inside as I slam the door shut behind us.

"Drop your purse, Tea," I command.

Her eyebrows pull together.

"Drop your goddamn purse. Don't make me repeat myself."

The purse falls to the floor as I sling my shades onto her dresser. I tear my cut off and let it drop to the floor. I don't have time for niceties. My demons beg me to rip into her, to punish her for something she doesn't even know she did wrong. My dark eyes narrow at her as I pull my belt from its loops.

"You have fifteen seconds to strip down to nothing but your bare skin. Time starts now."

When she makes no move to take her clothes off, I fold my belt in my hands and snap it. The sound echoes throughout the room. "The more you misbehave, the more pain you'll receive, Tea."

She has wanted this for so long, and now that I am about to give it to her, she acts hesitant and timid about the entire thing.

"I'm not asking again."

Tatiana's eyes widen when she realizes this isn't another one of my head games. This is me, about to own her. This is my dark side she has always wanted to taste. She kicks off her shoes as her shaking hands lower her skirt. Her peach colored skin calls to me. The things I am going to do with that fine body excite me. When her skirt is pooled at her feet, I peel out of my boots and jeans, never taking my eyes off her. A growl of ownership rises in my throat as my shirt joins the other clothes on the floor. When she lifts her blouse over her head, her peaked nipples beg my mouth to latch onto them with my teeth. All the will power I have left evaporates. It escapes me completely.

"Baby oil," I hiss. "Get me some, now!"

Tatiana's blonde hair bounces as she runs to her bathroom and returns with baby oil in her hand.

"Toss it on the floor. If I decide to go easy on you, it might come in handy." I lift a finger and motion for her to come near me, and her steps don't falter. When she stands in front of me, I swipe her hair behind her shoulder. "What's my color, baby?"

She gasps ever so lightly, bringing a devilish smirk to my face. "Your color or your scene color?"

Perceptive little lamb, isn't she? "Mine," I growl as I jerk her against my body. I run my nose along her jaw and whisper into her hair. "Mine." I breathe.

Her head tilts to the side as she answers. "Black, god, your color is black," she pants.

I pull back and stare at her. Get a fucking grip. She knows too much about you already. Take back control!

"Scene name," I growl.

Tatiana's body jerks backwards at the change in my tone of voice.

"Sage," she growls back at me, earning her an extra welt on that delicious skin of hers. I don't know if I like it, but it'll do for now.

"You are to call me Tavis and nothing else." I don't ask if she understands. In a way, I am testing her, testing the knowledge she thinks she already has. "If I need to stop, you call black, not red." Again, I don't ask. "So… you think you're a masochist, do you?" I murmur as I push her body slowly towards the bed.

"I don't think. I know." She glares at me.

Another strike is added onto her long list. "We'll see," I say as I jerk my head for her to climb onto the bed. "Sit on the edge, lie back, and stretch one leg to each post at the foot of the bed." I am about to see exactly how much pain she thinks she can handle. See how toned her body is for rigorous activities. When her pale, pink, polished toes rest on each pole and her face contorts a smidge, the evil bastard inside of me smiles in victory. As I move away, her eyes follow my toned chest while I open her closet door to look for anything I might use to tie her ankles. I chuckle when I see scarves hanging from a hook. She is making this entirely way too easy on me. I don't bother shutting it behind me as I walk back to her, fisting pieces of fabric between my fingers.

I wrap three of the colored scarves around my neck and wink at her as my fingers brush at one ankle. Her naked body rises and falls rapidly in anticipation of my next move, but she has no idea I'm playing with her. This is nothing like what she is about to experience.

When my long fingers clasp around her foot and jerk hard, she lets out a yelp. "Quiet." I chuckle as I tie the silk around her ankle twice, before bringing the fabric to the pole and securing her to it. I stride to the other side and repeat the process. The demons chuckle as her thigh muscles pulsate from the stretch. Satisfied the ties are tight enough that she can't pull loose, but slack enough for her to do what I need, I step back and admire her glistening pussy.

I snap my fingers as I bark at her. "Give me your hands, Sage!" I move forward to grasp her hands in mine, and slowly pull her up as she whines. "This is nothin, Darlin'." I drawl because it isn't. If she thinks her muscles are pulling right now, she has no idea what they are going to feel like in about five minutes. After the fabric slides as far as it can go against the skin of her ankles, and her feet are planted on the mattress, I climb up on the bed. I stand behind her and place my chin in the crook of her neck as she shivers against me. "Are you scared?"

"No, Tavis." Her body leans against mine.

Good girl. I don't do rewards, but if I did, she would have earned one. "You should be," I whisper into her ear as my hand trails lightly down her arm. I tilt back and ram my cock into the globes of her ass. "I'll ask again in a moment." When I move away from her body, she whimpers in protest, when really, she should be crying for release. She's a brave little morsel. I tie both arms to the poles, jump off, and move around the bed to see my handiwork. Not a bad job for being without my belongings.

She works her wrists, and the demons inside me smile in

triumph as she yanks and pulls. "Okay… so, maybe this isn't all that comfortable," she murmurs in a small, quiet voice.

My stance changes as I spread my legs, cross my arms over my naked chest, and glare at her. "I thought you could handle pain, Sage," I rumble. "If you can't handle this…" I trail off, and act as if I'm going to leave. This is absolutely nothing close to what I want to do to her. I hope to fuck she hasn't been teasing me. That will only anger me beyond control.

"No, no, I can handle it," she protests.

I chuckle, turn back around, and smirk at her. "What are you feeling?"

Her lips tilt into a seductive smile because she knows what I want. She knows the answer I crave. "Pain."

Uncrossing my arms, I stalk towards her and run my nose through the apex of her thighs, forcing her to moan. The sound of her melodic voice makes the skin of my balls tighten. It's time for me to cause some pain and pleasure.

***

Tatiana

When I found him pacing along the hallway, I never in a million years thought I'd end up tied, standing upright, to my bedposts. The silk pulls at my skin, and my muscles feel as if they will tear at any moment, and yet, even though it hurts so bad, it hurts so good. The longer I stay like this, the harder it burns, and the harder it burns, the more my juices flow uncontrollably down my legs. Jesus, who knew?

"Well, what do we have here," he mumbles into my pussy. The rumbles of his voice vibrate against my clit, and I moan. "You can't be getting off, darlin'. I need you fucking dry for this shit."

Oh, god. I can't help it, I want to scream, but deep down, I am scared. I refuse to show that weakness. I can't. I want him. So, I do the only thing I can do. I bow my head. "I'll try better, Tavis." God, that name makes me shiver.

"Good girl."

I shut my eyes at the sound of his drawl. There is no way I am going to be able to get through this without coming. The sound of his voice makes me want to squirt all over his tongue as he runs his nose up and down my lips. When he moves away from my thighs, I want to cry out in protest, but I don't. This is his show, and I so desperately want to take part in it.

"Open your eyes, Sage."

I do as I'm told, and when the light from a flickering candle bounces in my vision, my eyes dart to his, and the evil smirk I have come to love, lines his gorgeous face. How did I not even hear him light that? His words that he is dangerous play over and over again in my head.

He was trying to warn you, dumbass, and now look, the feel of his nose on your pussy makes you catatonic!

I bite my bottom lip, nodding that I give my permission. That is the reason he had me open my eyes. It is then I realize we

116

aren't doing a scene. He is testing my every limit, and that makes my heart pound against my chest a million miles an hour. Oh god. I look frantically around my room, trying to take inventory of all things he could use against me to cause pain, but I am coming up with a short list. When he chuckles, it breaks me out of my own head.

"Nothing in here is gonna save you, darlin'," he cackles.

My eyes dance to the candle and watch the wax melt and pool around the wick. He's letting it build, and the thought of hot wax pouring all over my skin causes the hairs on my body to stand at full alert. Shadow sets the candle on my dresser and moves to the door. Where the hell does he think he is going? Oh no, he is not leaving me here like this.

He opens the door and I panic. "Shadow, no! You can't leave me tied the fuck up!"

The door slams shut with him still in the room. "What the fuck did you call me?"

My eyes widen with his tone. Shit!

"Let me tell you somethin'. We may not be in a scene right now, but I gave two direct fucking orders. Repeat them for me now!" he roars.

I gulp and release air. "To call you Tavis and to use the color black."

Everything in me wants to argue that he didn't necessarily order me to use the color, but the look on his handsome, mean face keeps that argument locked down inside me.

"Yes, now shut the fuck up, for once."

Why is that turning me on, instead of pissing me off? While I am left questioning myself, he opens the door wide, right when

Smokey walks by.

Oh, fuck me sideways, really?

"What in the fuck?" Smokey questions, doing a double take.

How embarrassing is this shit.

Shadow chuckles before giving what may be an explanation to him, but not to me. "She wanted to play. Don't worry, she likes it. Watch her for me." He erupts in laughter as his naked ass takes off down the hallway.

He did not leave me naked, tied up, and with a sexy as hell Smokey staring at me!

That fucker knows it is only Smokey, Rap, and me on this floor. He did this shit on purpose. It is then that I realize I'm experiencing my first humiliating moment in the world of sadomasochism. That motherfucker!

Smokey leans against the doorframe and chuckles. "I must say, little Tea, that this is a sight to behold."

I groan. This moment hurts worse than the restraints on my limbs. "Oh, shut your cocky ass up."

And even though this moment is well beyond embarrassing, it has an intoxicating feel to it. From the fabric pulling on my legs, to the flickering candle flame, to the sexy as shit asshole standing at my door, everything about it screams hot.

Smokey lights a cig, and strolls right into my room to take a seat right in my bedroom chair.

Oh, hell no, this is not fucking happening.

"You can take your gorgeous, blond ass right on out of here." I try to move a finger and point towards the door. Fucking restraints!

"I don't think so, baby. You look mighty delicious, all restrained like that." He chuckles with his smoke hanging out of the corner of his mouth.

Shit! Why on earth do I find him so delicious? Smokey has always been sexy, but right here, right now, at this very moment, I am actually thinking about it. I can't be having this. My father would kill me if I allowed two members of Breakneck to fuck me at one time. That fantasy will have to be thrown out the window. But shit, with him staring at me like I'm his favorite brand of whiskey, it makes me want to rethink this entire situation I am in right now.

Smokey's eyebrows shoot up like he's read my thoughts, and I frown.

Asshole thinks he knows what I'm thinking. Okay, maybe he does, but still.

When I'm about to lose my cool, Shadow's naked ass strolls back into my room with a book bag hanging off his shoulder.

"She's a sight like that. Is she not." He chuckles to Smokey.

Smokey stands, clasps Shadow in a bro hug, and turns to take one last look before agreeing with Shadow. I want to yell, "You realize, you basically hugged it out with your brother's naked junk all up on you, right?"

"Shut the door, would ya?" Shadow laughs.

Smokey's laughter fills the hallway as the door closes behind him.

"I fucking hate you right now," I murmur in a low voice.

"I told you to shut the fuck up. Let's see what we have here in my bag of pain." He smiles at me as the satchel falls from his shoulders. The sound as he unzips it echoes in my ears.

"Humiliation, check," I smart off.

His hand stops moving in the open bag as his gaze flies to mine. "You fuckin' keepin' track now? If that's the case, I'm really gonna lay into your ass."

Why can't he gag me so I will quit smarting off?

"You want me to?"

Shit! I said that out loud.

I do my best to shrug.

The most sadistic smile warps across his face. His eyes darken. A growl escapes him as he reaches into his bag of tricks and pulls out a ballgag with leather straps. The sack drops to the floor, and he stalks me like a predator would his prey.

The bed dips behind me. His strong hands squeeze my cheeks together as he forces my head to the side.

"Stick your tongue out."

I don't question him. In the past half hour or so, I have learned my lesson with my humiliation moment, so I do as he orders.

His head drops down, and he draws my tongue into his mouth. He sucks on it like a blow pop before his tongue dives between my lips. His tongue against mine feels like velvet. He devours me, and when I moan, he growls and bites down on my tongue. I cry out, his mouth sucking my tongue once again. He repeats this process until my mouth dries out completely, and I am left panting and gasping for air. He doesn't let me get a breath before shoving the gag into my open mouth, running the straps around my head, and clasping them in the back.

"Your mouth is nice and dry, is it not? I imagine it feels like a desert. You feel like you're thirsting to death, don't you? You poor thing, I bet you'd like a glass of water right now, wouldn't you?"

When the bed dips and he stands in front of me again, I glare at him hard.

"Now, since I've gagged you, darlin', you can't safe word. Those holes in that gag are made for you to blow through. They make a whistling sound when you do. Blow three times to safe word. If you don't blow three times in a row, I'm going to assume it's pleasure whistling through. Understand?" He taps his chin as my eyes trail down the ripples of his rock hard abs, all the way to his flaccid cock. How in the shit is he still soft? I'm so damn wet. Oh god, now I'm even thirstier than I was before. This is so fucked up!

"Whistle through the gag three times, Sage, so I know you understand!" he snaps at me, bringing my eyes back to his. They're the darkest I have ever seen now. The black is invading the white of his eyes. I shiver as I blow air through the gag as he ordered.

"Mmmm…," he murmurs as he turns to pick up the candle, now with almost an inch of hot, liquid wax sitting at the top. "This is gonna hurt, not gonna lie to you. Be ready. Breathe slowly in and out as you shift through the pain. Make sure there is enough space between the breaths so that I don't think you're safewording."

I nod, because what else am I supposed to do. I can't fucking talk. When he looms in front of me, his tall form stands so that his mouth meets my tits. His velvet tongue flicks at one nipple before he pulls back to flick it with his free hand. I moan and the gag's whistle filters through the air. The wetness pools deeper between my thighs.

121

"I can smell you. Don't fucking come until I say you can, and that is a big fucking if tonight. Your attitude has pissed me off, and seeing you with him has lit me ablaze," he roars, his hot breath bouncing off of my skin.

So that is what this is about! He didn't fucking want me until he saw me with my ex? That little fucking prick son of a bitch!

I jerk my head to the side and stare at the wall. Fuck him. He isn't getting any more attention from me. A hard slap to my pussy draws my gaze back and has me crying out into the gag, and my eyes immediately water.

"Stop fucking pouting!"

I close my eyes, allowing them to clear before I reopen them. He seems appeased by this and walks around to the side of the bed and climbs up. From the corner of my eyes, I see him drop to his knees and move towards my backside, never once spilling the melted wax. "Take a breath, because it'll be your last free one."

Oh, god, what does that even mean?

His palm connects with my skin, and I scream against the ball in my mouth.

"I told you to take a breath. Next time, you'll listen to me," he drawls as his hand rains fire down on my ass cheeks.

I scream until my throat burns. I want to cry out, to ask him what in the hell he is doing, but he seems to read my mind. It's a good thing, too, because I'm left immobile because of him.

"What? You thought you were getting the wax? You silly girl." His sexy laugh washes over me as he stands. "Your skin is tender now," he whispers in my ear as the molten candle spills onto my back. A scream echoes throughout the room, a scream that sounds non-human, as the scalding liquid trickles down to the globes made raw with his palm. That scream came from me, and it continues as the wax pours evenly over my delicate skin.

I want so badly to whistle three times, but he will see me as weak, and I don't want that. I want all of him, so if I need to work myself up to his satisfaction, I will. I want this lifestyle, but more importantly, I want it with him.

My face heats and I know it is bright red as he coaxes me. "Breathe in…," he murmurs into my ear. "Breathe out." I do as I am told. "Again." My pulse slows as I repeat this process as ordered. "Good girl. You made it through a short course of wax play."

My head drops in relief, knowing that part is over, and he tucks my hair behind my ears while his body presses against my sore backside.

"Shh… calm, breathe one more time for me, baby."

My heart beats erratically at the softness of his tone, and I turn my head to the side to look directly into his soulless eyes. He blows out the candle and leans over to set it on my nightstand. His thumb reaches under my right eye and catches a lone tear I didn't know was escaping down my face. Shadow gives me a moment longer to stare into his eyes before he jumps down, picks up his bag, and digs through it.

Oh god, can I have five breathing minutes, please? I want to beg and whistle, but when I see his large cock begin to harden, I realize I have no choice but to go through with this. He truly requires pain. Until this moment, I didn't realize the extent of his need for it. This knowledge, this proof I now have, gives me the strength I need to let him move forward.

Shadow pulls out a bottle of mouthwash, twists the cap off,

swishes, and then swallows it. What in the world is he doing? He strolls over to the bed, bag in one hand, mouthwash in the other. He sets the sack down on the mattress and uses his free hand to twist my nipples in his callused grip. I don't dare scream. I absorb the pain like he wants, and as I want, too. After he is satisfied with himself, he pours the contents over my tweaked buds, and I hiss through the burning. His eyes flick to mine, and he smiles at me so warmly that it makes the searing pain fade away to nothing.

"You're astounding me, baby. I want you to know that everything that I'm pulling out of this bag is brand new. Fear nothing. Well… fear nothing but me, of course."

Those words cause me to whimper lightly around the gag.

He digs through the bag once again, and pulls out the strangest looking equipment I have ever seen. "This was all light. We're going dark now."

Oh, good god!

I look down at his cock and watch it rise as he sets up the strange machine. Fuck, he is serious! My bum is still on fire, and he wants something heavier?

"You're about to experience edgeplay. Whistle three times if you don't want this. Do it now."

My eyes widen, and he waits for my decision. Do I want this? Last time, I was nearly killed, and then I remind myself that was with a complete stranger. I trust Shadow. He will harm me, but he knows his limitations, and I have an out. He has made sure of this. With determination, I nod my head once.

***

(Part Two)

Tatiana

The panic inside me does not start until he pulls out a needle. That moment is when my breathing picks up and my skin heats. I tell myself to trust him, trust that he knows what he's doing, and trust him not to harm me in an everlasting, permanent way. The bag drops to the floor as he brings a metal clamp towards my right nipple. My eyes flick to his to get some kind of read off him. I can't. I come up empty, and I assume he is doing that on purpose. His left hand grabs my full tit, and the metal locks down hard on my nipple. Instead of a muffled cry, I moan. This seems to appease him as he repeats the process with my other tit. Once both of my nipples are clamped with the cold metal, he picks up the needle, brings it up to my left bud, and rams it in. This time there is no moan. It is nothing but a cry as the needle rips through me.

"Ohf… gawd," I mumble over the gag.

"One more, and then I'll take the ballgag out of your mouth."

I close my eyes and nod, right as the needle pierces through my other nipple. His reasoning for this is so unclear, but I know he has one.

"The little spurts of blood trickling from your delectable tits, make my cock rock-fucking solid, baby. Take a look," he murmurs.

My eyes fly open so that I can look down. His cock is so big that I muffle a moan, and the color turns a purple hue. While I gaze at his rigid erection, he unties my ankle and grips my foot, lightly twisting it to restore circulation. Once he is satisfied, he moves to the other. I know he is not finished with me. He has barely gotten started. The wetness between my legs grows heavier with the thought of more to come.

"Okay, baby, prepare yourself. The holes in your nipples will make them more sensitive to the electric stimulation you're about to undergo. The sore skin will heighten all of this."

Shadow picks up two long metal pieces connected to a small box and clamps them onto my nipples. Searing pain shoots through my chest. Once they are secure, he reaches down to the box and looks at me. "It's time to take you to a place you've never been before. I can't hold my demons off any longer." He sounds almost sad as he flips the switch. The machine sends an electric current humming through my body. I close my eyes, my moans caught and muffled behind the gag. He raises up on the bed to remove it from me, and tosses it to the floor. One hand wraps tightly around my neck as he positions his cock at the hole in my backside.

"Oh, god," I moan as the electric current picks up speed.

"Your muscles are beginning to spasm." He chuckles against my ear. "Unclench your ass. Oh wait, you can't," he hisses in my ear, as if the mere thought makes him the happiest man on earth. "My demons are about to claim this beautiful ass."

His words scatter in my brain as I spasm, but nothing could compare to the consuming pain that scorches through me, blistering every nerve in my body, when he rams his large, hard cock inside my ass. A scream tears from my throat as my ass feels as though it is being ripped in half.

"That was the scxiest fucking sound that I have ever goddamn heard," he growls while he thrusts into me. "I'm gonna make this hole bleed."

My mind clouds when his hand tightens around my neck. My nerve endings are attacked from different directions. My knees quiver, and my hands wrap around the bed posts as my entire body seizes. The surface of my skin heats, and then stings. My very breath drains from my body, taking me to a place where I feel as if I am floating on thin air. My grip on the beams of my bed loosens. Black dances behind my eyelids. My eardrums pound to a steady beat, his rhythmic thrusts in perfect timing with the sounds in my ears. The thought of a feather filters through my haze, and my body slumps backward onto a soft, pillowy type cloud. The voice of an angel speaks to me as the color returns to my world.

"Shhh… you did so fucking well, Tatiana. Fuck am I proud of you. Open those beautiful blue eyes for me."

My eyelids flutter a few times before they open. Oh. My. God. "Hi," I croak at him. The back of his hand runs over my cheek as I gain consciousness. "That… that was… that was amazing," I breathe, looking into his black eyes. "Did you release your demons?"

"I did," he drawls with a sexy smirk. "That is one of the ways to properly play with asphyxiation and electric stimulation. A very dangerous combination, and your very first real edgeplay experience. A few more minutes, and I could have killed you."

I gasp and try to sit up.

"No, baby, you're all kinds of loose. Don't move. Rest." He pushes me back down and reaches over to my nightstand to grab my hand mirror. "Not one single bruise," he says as he hands it to me.

I try to lift my arm, but it falls when it is halfway in the air. Shadow laughs, his body bouncing under mine as he holds the mirror in front of me. I can't believe it. The skin around my neck is a slight red, but there is no blue or black. I tilt my head back and look at him. "I have no words," I say as I wrap my hand around my neck. It is barely even tender to the touch. How in the hell did he do that? "When did you untie my hands and lay me down?"

"When you were in subspace. I must admit, Tea, I'm very pleased to learn that your mind trusts me enough for you to even go there with me." He looks extremely satisfied with the outcome of it all, so I smile at him. "You can do better than that," he teases me.

I can, but I am so damn sore. "I hurt," I mumble.

His lips press down on my forehead as he gently moves me onto the mattress, freeing his body from mine. "Close your eyes, darlin'. I'll take care of you," he murmurs as he gets up from the bed.

My eyes flutter for a few moments as he disappears into my bathroom, and that is the last thing I remember before succumbing to sleep.

***

Chapter Fifteen

The morning after

Tatiana

The morning light blazes through my open curtains. When I stretch, my sore muscles pull and force a yelp to escape me. I slap my hand over my mouth when I realize Shadow is still in my bed. Oh, shit. When I turn my head to look at him, he's awake and staring at me with a look I don't quite understand. It is blank. Great, watch him start the whole spiel of why this was a mistake. Blah, blah, and more blah. I climb out of bed as he begins to sit up. Hell no, I'm not about to get the dreaded morning after talk. I have never had one, and I don't plan on ever having one. This fucker has turned me into a kinky one-night stand. If only I could get away with kicking him in the balls.

"Morning, darlin'," he drawls in a sexy voice as he yawns. His stretch reveals his delicious, muscular physique.

I scramble over to my dresser, open the pajama drawer, and throw on some sweats and a tank before I turn to face him. When I do, his face is laced with that sexy smirk he is so good at doing. It makes my heart beat jump, and I hate it. I fucking hate it!

"Mornin'," I mumble as I all but run to my bathroom to brush my teeth and hair. I must look like a tragic mess, and my ass fucking hurts! He could have used some lubricant or something. Shit. And then, I remember this is what I wanted. This is what I want to teach my body. The thought of learning how many spurts of pain I can handle excites me, and I grin in the mirror as I remember the all mighty high I got last night. The feeling is addictive, and now that I think about it, I crave more of it, but I will not dare let Shadow know this. He's about to give me the speech, and I am not humiliating myself by asking him for more of what happened last night. I'll wait, learn more, and seek it from someone else. I need to stop this hanging on by a thread feeling he gives me. Yesterday morning, I had forgotten all about him while having breakfast with Haden. I need to have more mornings like that one.

I leave the comfort of my bathroom, and Shadow still hasn't moved. Okay, what do I do with this? He is trying to stay comfortable before reminding me that we can't let something like last night happen again.

"Have a handful more nights like last night, darlin', and you'll be ready to scene for real."

Seriously! What a fucking jerk! He fucked the shit out of my ass last night, and he's already talking about me doing scenes with other men? Jesus! Could he make me feel more like a slut?

"Gee, thanks, that gives me the warm fuzzies," I smart off. "My pussy tingles at the thought of other men doing what you did to me last night. Seriously. I'm dripping wet," I purr sarcastically.

If he can be a prick, I can be a bitch as well.

Shadow sits up all of a sudden with a confused look on his face.

"I wonder if I could get two different men to do me at the same time." I pretend to enjoy the very idea of it, even though I already know it isn't for me. "Damn, I can't wait for the club to take over Euphoria."

He hops up from my bed, shaking his head back and forth as if he is confused at my sudden behavior. It is a show. He's going to use my attitude as his excuse.

Come on, Shadow, give it to me so I can forget all about this shit.

"Tea, what the fuck is going on with you this morning? I'm startin' to think I gave you brain damage last night."

What in the freaking, flippity fuck!

"What?" I ask in disbelief. He can't be serious. I think my mood is very normal for this type of situation. I have never had a one-night stand. I don't count the asshole that almost killed me. I'm distancing myself from him with this conversation. Isn't that what he planned to do as well? Tell me how it shouldn't have happened, and how we can't let it happen again? I'm so confused.

"You're kinda bein' a bigger bitch than normal," he says while putting on his jeans.

I can't even enjoy the sight of him being naked and out of the bed. I should be able to appreciate watching him get dressed. Instead, I'm still hanging onto the bitch comment.

"I never knew you thought I was a bitch." Wow. I can't even be around him after that comment.

His mouth opens and shuts several times before he can back himself out of the hole he dug. "I didn't mean it like that!"

How else am I supposed to take that comment?

"Look, I am starving. Get your shit, and get out of my room. Last night was fun. Thanks for taking me on a ride of a lifetime." I smart off and wink as I flee from my room, leaving an open-mouthed Shadow behind me.

When I get downstairs and turn the corner to the kitchen, Winter is already sitting at the table. She must be the only one up beside Shadow and me right now. Usually the kitchen is bustling with people if they aren't hung-over. I study her, noticing she looks a bit pale. It worries me.

"Umm… Win… don't take this the wrong way, but you look sick."

She nibbles the toast that is on the plate in front of her. "I haven't been feeling all that great. Pregnancy hasn't been kind to me," she answers with a sad tone that breaks my heart.

I move to the cabinets, grab a glass, get the orange juice out of the fridge, and pour her a glass. "Drink this," I say as I hand it to her. "You should have already had a glass this morning."

"Thanks. I think since I can't keep my food down, it's messing with me." Her hand shakes as she reaches for it.

That's understandable. Throwing up so much is hard on a woman, let alone a pregnant woman. I don't really know if orange juice is good for pregnant women, but I know it makes me feel brand new if I have a glass every morning.

"Honestly, I haven't been sleeping very well, and Braxx has been on edge since the day with the gun bullshit, and now this BDSM takeover. I know he's worried, and I don't want him to know that his stress is stressing me out."

I listen to her. Winter doesn't open up much about what goes on between her and Godfather. I get it, though, because they're married. You don't go sharing all your private feelings and emotions about something so personal.

"Stop stressing, Win. It'll all be okay. I stopped worrying about lockdowns, takeovers, and all the other bullshit that comes along with being in an MC family, months ago. I got tired of it ruling my life. You need to stop letting this get to you, especially with you being pregnant."

She looks at me, and I mean really looks at me, before smiling. "You've grown a lot over the last six months, Tea."

My lips pull into a grin. "I know," I say with a wink before pouring my own orange juice. I was so worried about her that I forgot to make myself one.

"Honestly, everything will be okay." I open the cabinet and grab a glass while peering around the cabinet door. "You'll see."

When she gets up to put her plate into the dishwasher, she stops and stares at me. "You're glowing."

Shouldn't I be the one saying that to a pregnant woman? Even though I have that thought, and even though Shadow ruined it this morning, I find myself cheesing like crazy at her comment.

"Last night…" I shake my head. "Shadow and I—"

I don't go any further. I let her pick up on it.

"Really?" she asks in disbelief.

"Yeah, it was fantastic," I whisper. "But he ruined it this morning by trying to hit me with the morning after talk. I cut out quickly before he could."

She smacks me playfully on the arm. "Well, at least you got some."

We start to laugh. God, it feels good to do that freely and not have to force it. Our laughter stops when, on the kitchen monitor hanging under the wall cabinets, we see a taxi pull up to the gate.

"Who could that be?" We say at the same time with confused faces. When a blonde haired woman steps out of the cab, Winter gasps.

"It's my sister. At least I think it is," she says as she bends to get a better look at the monitor. "Yeah, it's her. I video chatted her last week. What in the hell is she doing all the way here in the United States? My husband is going to flip the fuck out. We have too much shit going on for more company. We're already hosting Akela. Dammit!"

I follow her through the compound parking lot to the gate. This is unfuckingbelievable.

"Mace, hit the gate button," she says to my brother who is on night watch duty.

"I was about to."

When the gate slowly opens, Winter stands there as her sister comes into view. For someone who has only video chatted and never met her sister in person, Winter doesn't appear to be too happy. I have no idea what is going on with her lately. She is not acting like herself right now.

"Sabine, what in the hell are you doing here?"

The blonde's smile fades. Winter's tone shocks her, but it shouldn't. It is beyond rude to fly across the world and show up unannounced. At least Akela had a reason to come here. She hadn't heard from her sister, and it worried her.

"Hello to you too, sister," Sabine answers, her heavy accent lacing her English words.

From here, I can tell Winter is rolling her eyes at her sister as she palms her slightly swollen stomach. Something is definitely going on with her. She is usually friendlier than this and for seeing her sister for the first time in person unannounced or not she is acting cold and that is not Winter like behavior.

"If you must know I was involved in a scandal and our mother sent me here until it blows over," she huffs out, rolling her suitcases into the compound. How long does she expect to stay here? By the looks of her bags, you'd think it was months!

"I don't understand, she couldn't send you somewhere else? This is a really bad time."

I agree with Winter on this point. Right now, the club is under an enormous amount of stress. The last thing we need is for the reporters to get wind that a princess is laying low in our compound, especially when we have who knows how much illegal shit going on.

"No, the media has no idea you even exist to me. This is the safest place she could send me without word spreading around."

I find that hard to believe. Of all the places in the world, *this* was the only location?

"Where is our mother?" Winter asks as the gate closes.

"She'll be here after a little cleaning up behind me, and when she knows for sure no one is paying attention to her movements."

Her presence is going to irritate a lot of people, and to be honest, I don't want Sabine anywhere near my uncles or Shadow. She looks like trouble to me. I have no desire to be around when she tells Godfather, so I stay outside when they go into the live-in. He's going to be so damn pissed.

135

***

Chapter Sixteen

Shadow

I wish the fuck I could leave the compound. When Winter announced her sister's arrival, I thought the Prez would come unglued. We don't need any attention right now. Even Winter doesn't want her sister here. With the BDSM takeover, we have enough to keep us busy, without some bitch with royal blood showing up and making us worry about the media raining hell down on us.

Akela's quiet nature doesn't bother the Prez, and she appears to be helping Pyro in ways that his brothers cannot. When Sabine showed up this morning, it put every single one of us in a foul mood, and Tatiana is taking her presence harder than the rest of us. Every time she is a few feet from Sabine, Tea glares at her as if, at any moment, she is going to cause her bodily harm. I have tried to approach her about it, and when I go near her, she turns that glare on me.

So, yeah, I am not proud to be waiting in Tatiana's bedroom, but I need fucking answers from her. I thought we were good. That everything was washed away. From the way Tea has been acting, it's apparent this issue needs to be resolved.

Sitting in a chair by her bed, I flash back to our sexy as fuck time together, and again, I wonder why the fuck she left in such a rush. She won't talk to me about it. For someone who wanted so bad for me to fuck her, I wouldn't have thought she would have run off like that this morning. Her behavior, hell, everyone's behavior these past few weeks has been confusing as hell. When I add in our unlikely guests, things seem way too weird for my liking.

My leg bounces up and down as I grow impatient as fuck waiting for her. When she finally enters the room and slams the door behind her, I feel some sort of relief.

"What in the fuck are you doing in my room?"

Jesus, what's with all the hostility with her?

"We need to talk," I say.

"We ain't got shit to talk about." She throws her purse onto her bed and her keys on her dresser.

A deep scowl forms on my face. I was inside her last night, and now, she acts as if I am some stranger who's annoying the shit out of her. Never in my life has a woman behaved like this towards me. It is all kinds of fucked up.

"Tea, what is wrong with you? I had your naked body pressed all up on me last night!"

She grabs the bottom hem of her shirt and rips it off with such an attitude, it would turn me on if she wasn't acting like such a cold hearted bitch. It's as if she considers me some nasty ass, one night stand.

When she turns to walk away, I jump out of the chair and grab her elbow, spinning her back around to face me. "You don't get to treat me like this after last night. Don't fucking be like this. I gave you what you fucking wanted, goddammit!"

My blood beats hot as my mind drifts to spanking the shit out of her.

"I got what I wanted," she hisses, jerking her arm from me. "We fucked. It was amazing, but now, I can cross it off my to-do list!"

My hand falls to my side as I stare at her retreating into the bathroom. Did I get dismissed? What in the fuck? She used me? That shit is so damn laughable. If she wants to act like this, and she doesn't want to let me get a word in edgewise about what occurred between us, then fine. I can't have a conversation with someone who is unwilling, and to be honest, I'm mentally exhausted. She always says I'm the one that plays fucking head games. As I walk out of her room, I snort a laugh. Head games, my ass. I want to continue what we started last night, but if she wants to be a bitch, she can fucking kiss my tanned southern ass. Ain't no piece of pussy worth this damn migraine and frustration.

I dig my phone out and check the time. I have a few minutes before our church meeting starts, so I light a smoke and make my way to the clubhouse. After Sabine's arrival, Prez called it, and we expect it won't be a pleasant one.

Before I walk in the chapel door, Winter stops me. "Gun." She holds out her hand.

Well, this I agree with. I lift my pant leg to unstrap my holster, pass that one to her, and then remove the one from the back of my jeans and give that to her as well. She hands them to Mace Jr., and he puts them in a new safe built into the wall next to the chapel doors. Well, someone has been busy.

"When the gavel slams at the close of the meeting, you'll get them back."

Well, fuck me running. Is the Prez finally taking control of his club again? I sure the hell hope so. This shit had started to get messy.

I ignore my Prez's scowl because I know it isn't intended for me. By adjusting my dick before I sit, I give the impression I was off getting some ass. I mean, I was trying to set up some regular pussy, but Tatiana seems to have grown a new head over the past few hours. *Fuck her!*

Stop thinking about how good it felt when her asshole strangled the shit out of your cock. She's acting like a bitch. Oh, but fuck me sideways if it didn't squeeze me good. The thought of sticking a plug in her ass and pounding into her pussy while she's bound is glorious. Shit, why is it I want to start this, but now she doesn't? I will never fucking understand women.

"Earth to fuckin' Shadow, where the fuck is your head? I've been talkin' for five goddamn minutes!" My Prez roars out as he throws his lighter against the table.

Ah, hell.

I'm not about to tell my Prez, in front of Tatiana's father, no less, that I was thinking how good her pussy would feel on my dick if I plugged her ass to apply extra pressure.

"What in the fuck, Shadow!" ZZ yells as he slams his fist against the table.

Ah, dammit. Not again.

"What'd you say about my daughter's ass?"

Ah, shit!

"Brother… don't ask," Smokey interrupts.

As Tea would say, fuck a motherfucking flying duck!

"Man, look, she don't want me no more. Let me have my thoughts in peace. Sorry they were out loud." I mean, what else can I say? That couldn't have been easy for a father to hear. Right?

The room booms with questions, and I ignore all but one.

"What are your intentions?" ZZ asks, his voice eerily calm but his stare directed sternly right at me.

Well, they were to strap your daughter up, hurt her, and fuck her so many damn times my cock would fall off, but don't worry about that. She doesn't want shit to do with me after I've done fucked her ass, and hard, too.

"Nothing now. She made that clear," I grumble.

"Maybe the next time, you'll try." ZZ laughs and shakes his head.

If he knew what I did to his daughter last night, I sure the fuck don't think he'd be so cool with me right now. Is he fucking nuts? I should tell him exactly how it went down, and maybe he won't be so quick to approve of our non-existent relationship.

"All right, enough of this bullshit. We have an unwanted fuckin' visitor, and it pisses me off. The only thing that pisses me off more is my wife being upset, and she is fucking pissed. I want Sabine watched so fucking close, you're sittin' on her ass when she squats to piss! Is that clear," Prez seethes out, his teeth clattering together as his jaw works back and forth.

This is what the brothers and I expected, so no one says shit.

"Now, unfortunately, I gotta go handle Shadow's dumbass, fuckhead friend who doesn't know how to handle his own trade, so that means Pyro has to stay here to manage the women. Everyone, including Akela, has been off since Sabine's arrival. We may not know Akela that well, but I do know that I invited her to stay, and you know how I feel about my guests."

Yes, we do. When a guest is invited to stay at the club, it is serious business. Because of the illegal shit we do and the things we talk about, it isn't taken lightly.

"Not to mention, Sabine is of royal blood and she's stirred up a shit storm in her own country. I don't think I need to tell y'all this, but fuck do we need to watch our backs when it comes to her being here. Pyro, keep an eye on everything while I'm gone, and keep Akela company and away from the claws I sense on Sabine. I don't want our guest feelin' threatened at all. If I have to tell you that Akela is more important to my wife than her own sister is, then you don't know my wife. She doesn't know Sabine like she knew Lana, and if we know anything about Lana, it's that she came from good people. Will it be a problem?"

I know I'm not the only one holding my breath, awaiting Pyro's answer. He's in a tough spot. Keeping Akela company has to be hard on him because of her resemblance to Lana. I wouldn't want to be him, that is for sure.

"I'm good, Prez."

I bet he is anything but that.

"Okay, Sniper, Shadow, and Smokey, you're with me. The rest of you stay here. Piper, Storm, and especially my wife aren't to go into work until after the meeting and my say so."

My gut tosses and turns as the gavel bangs on the wood.

***

We aren't in Club Sated ten minutes before Alec strolls in with some big ass, fucking men. I mean men so fucking huge, they must've grown up eating goddamn Wheaties!

"Well, look who's done his fucking homework," Prez growls without standing up. He doesn't greet the bastards. Alec might have three scary fuckers with him, but we have Smokey and Sniper standing back. Sniper isn't called that just for the hell of it. He's earned his name.

"When you get a whiff of Breakneck MC having a problem, you gather insurance. Lucky for me, your insurance was in the newspaper months ago in the form of the Russians."

That smug ass, sorry, son of a bitch! I knew I smelled grey!

"Having to gather insurance speaks highly of us, man. I appreciate it." Prez chuckles and looks back at Smokey and Sniper in the background. "I happen to have my own," he says as he points to our brothers. "That blond man is my brother, Sniper. I don't have to tell you that his name means something."

Alec goes to sit in our booth, and the Prez stops him right in his tracks. "Don't bother. You won't be here long."

I chuckle. This is the Prez that gets my respect. Good to see he is back.

"Here's how this works. It's real simple. I want something, I take it, but I'm a business man after all, and I can negotiate. In a way." He smirks and shrugs his shoulders. "I'll give you five hundred thousand dollars for your club, right now. I know it seems like a small offer, but if you don't take it, that offer goes to less than pennies. You get me?"

The Russians' stance stiffens as Alec replies to my Prez. "You must be outta your fucking mind if you think I'm selling my club, much less giving it to you."

Jesus. You dumbfuck.

"Suit yourself. Go gather some more Russians, cause your ass is gonna need them here real soon." He points to the door. "Now get your fuckin' ass outta my wife's club."

They don't move until they hear Smokey and Sniper cocking their guns. Prez lets out a roar of laughter when Alec flinches. "You pussy, take your bodyguards and get the fuck outta here before I let my brothers rain fire on your dumbass!"

When they attempt to be casual and stroll out the way they came in, it shows a sign of weakness to us. Even with four of them, they are scared of the four of us. They should be. We've killed close to thirty people in the last year alone. That should make the motherfuckers piss themselves in cowardice.

"Angel is gonna be fuckin' pissed that the Russians are back. I thought we had handled them fuckers. Someone in the mob is still holdin' a damn grudge, because they wouldn't be here if not. More importantly, he got that info from somewhere other than the papers."

I agree. He couldn't get in contact with our enemies from reading a newspaper clipping. He got that information from someone else.

"Keep one patched member on each woman that leaves the compound. I don't think they'll go after them because of what happened the last time, but just to be safe."

Motherfucking Christ. Tatiana is already pissed off, and this shit is just going to make it worse. She isn't speaking to me, and once she hears this news, she is going to be extra bitchy. She hates, and I mean hates, being escorted, but the words that come out of my mouth are still... "I'll watch Tea."

Dammit!

"I figured as much," Prez says as we gear up and leave.

***

Chapter Seventeen

Tatiana

I can't believe I'm stuck with Shadow as my Patch escort. After what happened between us, I don't know how I feel about him watching my every move, and me knowing he's doing it. It is different when I can't see him, but when he is right there in my face, all up in my shit, how am I supposed to get over what happened between us? I think my Godfather hates me. That is the only explanation I have. He said Braxxon ordered him to keep watch on me, and if I know my Godfather, that is only partial truth. If he knew I didn't want Shadow around me right now, then he wouldn't be. And I have half a mind to fucking let him know I don't want Shadow within a hundred miles of me. I was supposed to meet Haden for lunch today, but no, as soon as I get up this morning, here comes Shadow with a grin on his face.

A fucking grin! As if this shit is at all funny, and to top it off, Winter is whispering about Russians.

But even though I have this fine ass, southern guy following my every move, it isn't going to stop me from seeing Haden. He needs a friend right now, and I am that friend for him. If I am being honest with myself, I need him just as much. I love my family, and I hate to admit, I even love Shadow, but I need a friend that doesn't know half of what is going on so I can get it off my mind.

When I smirk and let Shadow know where we are headed, I expect a pissed off look. Instead, he eyes the shit out of that ho, Sabine. It infuriates me because, even though I understand him pretty well, I can't read what the hell he's thinking when he does this shit in front of me. It proves that I made the right call to ignore his it was a mistake speech the other morning. I am so glad I didn't put myself through all that shit. A person can only take so much rejection and hurt. I am young, beautiful, and open to trying new things. He'd be lucky to have me. So with my blood on fire and my even more new determination, I plan to leave this fucker in his own shadow.

As he drives to Ma and Pop's, I refuse to speak to him for two reasons. First, he didn't hide the fact that he was checking out Sabine, and that is fucking bullshit. And two, instead of allowing me the freedom to walk down the street to the restaurant, he insisted he drive my damn car.

The vehicle isn't even in park when I throw open my door and rush inside. He knows better than to yell for me to stop. The confusion I'm feeling over the bullshit between us makes me furious, and the fact that it bothers me so much makes me even angrier. I deserve better than this bullshit.

So what does a girl do when she wants to get out from under a guy? I'll tell you what. She gets under another one. And what better way to do that than fuck an ex she's already been with.

I have never been more excited to see Haden waiting on me than I am in this moment. A chair screeches behind me as Shadow takes a seat, and I hurry towards my glorious ex-boyfriend. When he stands like a gentleman to greet me, it makes me even more dead set to fuck him while Shadow is around. I grab Haden's hand in mine and take off towards the women's bathroom with a protesting Haden dragging behind me.

"Woah, babe, what's going on?"

I jerk him through the door, shut it behind us, and move a big metal trashcan in front. It won't stop anyone from entering, but it sure as shit will alert me if someone tries.

"I need to fuck," I growl as I grab his shirt and push him into the nearest stall. "I need it so bad, it hurts." Okay, it really doesn't, but I wish it did. God, I wish I hurt right now.

"This isn't like you," he mumbles as my lips descend on his. "Dammit, babe!" he shouts and pushes me away. "Tell me what the fuck is going on, and I won't mind helping you with your little problem. But only if you tell me the damn truth right now!"

Sighing, I lean against the side of the stall. "I'm on partial lockdown again. I'm so fucking tired of men ruling my life, and for once, I want to make my own damn decision. I didn't know that my one decision would deny me."

Haden pulls me into the tightest hug I have ever been in, and holds me while tears spill down my cheeks. "You need a friend, babe, not a fuck," he murmurs into my hair.

I lose it, because I miss this part of us the most. Even when Haden was a douche, he knew me, and his words prove he still does. "I also know you well enough to know that look of love on your face, and it isn't directed at me, babe." I cry harder against his chest. "You're in love with that guy back there, aren't you?"

At this point, I sob uncontrollably into his shirt while he comforts me. "Yes," I choke out.

"Look, this is what I know about you when you love a person, Tatiana. You love so damn hard, and you don't ever give up on that person. You only gave up on me because I screwed up bad. I cheated, but deep down, you know it ran deeper. You knew it was because I couldn't handle your lifestyle. I'm so damn ashamed to admit it, but I was a pussy, and I needed to feel as loved as you did, at the time."

"That man out there is just plain stupid if he doesn't love you back. You deserve so much, and I sure know he looked pissed when I turned my head to look at him when you were dragging me off. That look was the look of straight up jealousy. If you listen to anything I say, listen to this. He lives the lifestyle you have grown up in. He understands it far better than anyone else could. So, if you're thinking about asking me for advice, listen to everything I said." He chuckles into my hair and pulls my face up to look at him. "And listen to this, too. Know that I think you're foolish if you give up on him. Men are stupid. Yes, I'm admitting that for all of us. We do stupid stuff. We don't admit our feelings until it is too late or close to being too late." He murmurs, his hands squeezing my cheeks with each point he tries to stress.

"So dry off that beautiful fucking face that I fell madly in love with when we were kids, finger brush that hair like you girls do, and get out there and show him what he's missing." He laughs before ruffling my hair. "Hell, on second thought, clean up your face. Let him think that I fucked you in this bathroom. It might stir up some good for your situation."

As I back up, I look at his shirt and see snot all over it. How embarrassing. "I'm so sorry about that." I point as I wipe my nose with the back of my hand. This is gross. Last year, I would have cried myself to sleep if Haden saw me like this. How the tables have turned.

"I have another one underneath it. You should know this." He smirks as he lifts his tee to reveal a plain white one.

"You Hanes lover." I laugh as I back out of the stall, walk to the sink, and turn it on to let the water heat so that I can wash my face. Warm water always feels good on my swollen eyes when I cry. "I swear, you better stay in contact when you go back to school." I say as I wet a paper towel to clean my face, and he tucks his other shirt in his back pocket.

149

"You wanna fuck with him some more?"

Of course I do. He eyed Sabine like he wanted to do with her what he did with me, and that breaks my damn heart.

"Yep."

"Good, I'll rumple this tee up as you wash your face."

I smile in the mirror as I wipe my ruined mascara away. "I love you, Haden. I do."

Haden stops pulling his tee in all directions, "I love you, too, babe. Always will."

When I'm satisfied with my appearance, he decides the appropriate amount of time has passed. We walk towards the door, but before I move the trashcan, I freak out.

"Fuck, this is gonna sound crazy, but you need to bite me hard on the neck, if this is going to work!"

Haden makes a what the fuck face and mouths the words at the same time.

"Fuck, I've been introducing myself to the world of masochism, and he knows this. I like pain, no, I love pain, when I'm being fucked. You need to bite me!"

Haden grabs my cheeks hard. "Are you telling me you've turned into a kinky little witch, and I passed on that shit," he says with a serious face. I almost feel bad for the guy. "Motherfucking hell, I have a feeling that I'll regret telling you no later on in my life. In fact, my cock is already starting to scream at me. How do I know if I bite too hard or not hard enough?"

Hmm… he took that news easily. "Until I say so. Bite so that you leave a lasting mark and almost draw blood. You can draw blood if you want, but we're in a hurry here."

He shakes his head like he can't believe he is about to do this, tilts my head to the side like a vampire readying his victim, and sinks his teeth into my neck. I let out a loud moan, and he groans, pushing me against the trashcan, and we almost tumble to the floor. His mouth never leaves my neck, and he bites me so hard, my pussy clenches. This moment lets me know I will always like pain. When my ex bites me on the neck and makes my legs tremble and moans escape me, I need no further proof. Shadow isn't the cause of these new feelings that have come over me. It is the pain itself.

Minutes go by before I push him away, panting from him getting me so worked up.

"That was so fucking badass!"

I smirk at him as I gain control over myself. "It's hot, right," I breathe as I move the trashcan out of the way. "You should experience it during sex. It is unfuckingbelievable."

"I must say that I like this grownup you a lot more every second."

I punch him on the arm as he opens the door for us.

"Game on," I hiss with a smile.

Oh, what I would give to be in Shadow's head right now.

When we get in the hall, we stop dead in our tracks at the scowling Shadow, standing there with a beet red face.

"You, get the fuck out of here before I slam your brains into that wall behind you," he hisses to Haden.

Who the hell does he think he is?

"Look, man, no hard feelings." Haden laughs him off. "She and I are becoming friendly again, is all."

I inwardly snicker. Love this guy!

"Take care of that love bite, babe, and call me later since your shadow," he air quotes, "is forcing us apart."

I lean in and wrap my arms around his neck, whispering a thank you. "I'll call you later. Love you."

My first love chuckles as he walks away from me, and Shadow grabs my arm and jerks me against him.

"When I take that pussy of yours, I swear to god I'm going to make it bleed!" he growls into my ear. "You thought your ass hurt, I'll show you hurtin'."

That should terrify me, but it only turns me on. *Fuck!* I jerk away from him.

"That's the thing. You are. Never. Touching. Me. Again." Since Haden has left, I forget all about getting lunch and walk towards my car.

Think on that, you Sabine-loving asshole!

***

Chapter Eighteen

Shadow

No words! None fucking at all for the way she treated me at the restaurant. What in the fuck did I do to make her go and fuck that dipshit! I wanted more. Isn't that what all chicks want? Shit, I was ready to hand my relationship balls over to her. I was ready to hurt her and no-one else. I haven't committed to a female since I was a teenager. And here is Tatiana, a woman who wanted me so fucking bad a few months ago, and who finally got me this week, and now she won't even let me get a word in edgewise. I don't understand this shit!

What in the fuck did I do wrong? I took care of her afterwards, stayed in bed with her, and woke up beside her the next morning. Isn't that what you're supposed to do when you want more than hot kinky sex?

When I see my Prez, I decide I need to clear my head of all Tatiana related things. The best way I know how is to stay the fuck away from her confusing ass.

"I don't want to follow Tatiana anymore," I say in an aggravated tone.

It isn't until the Prez doesn't say anything that I truly look at him. "What happened?"

He shakes his head as he pulls out his phone and hammers out a text. "I have to take Winter to the hospital. Something isn't right."

Oh shit! Not good.

"Look man, we knew this could happen. We didn't want to talk about it, and fuck, I still don't want to talk about it." The Prez drops his head as he finishes typing the text. "She had so much scar tissue from the rape that they didn't think she could handle a pregnancy this soon. Goddammit! I gotta go. Tell no one, cause we aren't for sure, but we have an idea. I shot Pyro a text. Go make sure he got it. If not, tell him to give me a call. Winter is waiting in the Rover."

What in the fuck do I say to that? There isn't anything I can say. Fuck, hasn't she been through enough shit already. Haven't we all! There is some seriously messed up karma working on this club. The women are cursed for loving a bunch of fucked up men. I can't even imagine what it must be like to worry if the baby your wife is carrying inside of her has died.

I scrub my face and let out a roar towards the sky. Emotional pain has never, and I mean never, fucking pleased me. It is messed up, considering I love inflicting physical pain, but this shit hurts even my heart.

I spot Pyro and open my mouth to speak, but he holds up his phone. The look on his face is the saddest I have ever seen, even worse than after Lana passed away. He got the message. Fuck did he get the message. When a member of our family hurts, we all hurt.

I turn away and cross the parking lot towards the clubhouse building. I need a stiff drink. We're on lockdown, and since I know Pyro and Sniper will be guarding this place, I am getting drunk. Not only do I have my Prez and my first lady's hurt laced inside my heart, I think the other pain I am trying to mask is seeing Tatiana walking out of that bathroom with that asshole with the scorching hot red bite mark on her neck.

Oh yeah, I need a drink or ten. This is not something I am used to feeling at all. It isn't jealousy. This is straight up caring. I think I want Tea in more than a friendship way, and I don't know what to do with that shit since she won't even speak to me. With the club on lockdown, some Russians in town, Winter possibly losing the baby, and the damn club takeover, I don't have time to be discovering these feelings right now. I reach for the moonshine instead of bourbon because fuck do I need something that will straight up make me forget right now. One hundred proof moonshine is the key to getting to the ignorance I so desperately crave.

I pop the cap and chug. It burns its way down my throat into the pit of my stomach. I sputter as I pull the bottle away. Shit! Oh, I am going to be lit up like a campfire.

"Can I have some of that?"

I turn towards the voice, my vision blurred, as my senses fight to recover from the rush of burning heat.

Dammit! I want peace right now!

"Sure, but if you get stupid and drink yourself to death, I ain't helping you."

The blonde, beautiful, evil bombshell smirks at me. "I think I'd know my limits," she flirts with her thick accent.

She needs to leave. She is barking up the wrong motherfucking tree. Tea already busted my ass for checking her out, and now that I seriously think about it, I think that is exactly why she let that fucker fuck her in the bathroom. Oh, hell no, really? Did I cause that shit?

Fuck no, I'm not!

155

"Get your own!" I growl. "You should be worried about your sister and not worried about drinking." My words slur. *Oh yeah, that's the spot*, I think as I gulp more of the fire down.

The blonde devil puts her hand on her hip and cocks her head. "Whatever. She has been a bitch since I arrived. If she wanted me to worry about her, she should have been more welcoming."

I don't understand half of what she says because of her accent, but I know that whatever that bullshit is that came out of her mouth is pathetic and cruel.

"You need to take your sorry ass on outta here, because you did not say that shit about our first lady!" Tatiana yells in anger.

My eyes dart to Tatiana. Where did she come from?

"Grow up, child." Sabine spouts at Tea.

I groan, tip the bottle to my lips, and gulp some more before I slam the decanter down on the counter, dig out my cell phone, and type an SOS to ZZ. I can't handle them both with all this shit I just poured down my throat floating around in my system. When I set my phone down on the bar, things only escalate, and I thank my balls that I sent out a text.

"Grow up? Bitch, please, I am grown. At least I ain't some spoiled little princess with the worst accent I have ever fucking heard, who had to run to my sister who barely knows me so I could escape a scandal because I slept with a married fucking man!"

That's the scandal that drove her to the United States? Really?

"Who the—? Never mind, I know who told you."

Tea smirks at Sabine as ZZ stomps into the clubhouse. "What the fuck is going on in here?"

156

Thank fuck, I really didn't want to get clawed to death in a cat fight.

"This child of yours needs to learn how to speak."

Sabine keeps digging herself a hole, doesn't she?

"My child needs to learn how to speak? Oh, this, bitch, I gotta hear." ZZ crosses his arms, daring Sabine to continue.

We watch as her mouth opens and closes while her mind works to find a response. She comes up empty handed, probably because ZZ looks like he wants to snap her head off her neck.

"My daughter graduated with a 4.2 GPA. What the fuck did you graduate with?"

A chuckle bursts through my drunken haze.

"I was homeschooled."

Tatiana loses it and doubles over as ZZ cackles evilly at Sabine's response.

"Homeschooled children aren't stupid, so I wonder who the fuck was teaching your ass. The nursery rhymes in children's books, perhaps?"

Never fuck with a man's child.

"What's going on here?" Mace Jr. asks while striding in with a confident look on his face.

"Your dad was insulting me," Sabine purrs.

Wait a damn minute here. With his confidence and her purring… oh, fuck no! It hasn't even been 48 hours! How in the hell did she sink her teeth in him that quickly?

"ZZ…," Mace Jr. questions. "What happened?"

ZZ looks to his son and then back to Sabine. I see the immediate realization of what I just put together come across his face.

"You didn't sleep with this bitch, did you, son? I mean, yeah, she's fine as fuck, but she even smells like a cunt!"

Mace Jr. frowns at his dad as he motions for Sabine to come to him. Seriously! I repeat, less than 48 hours!

"Son, you're making a huge fuckin' mistake here."

He doesn't look at his dad as he escorts the evil cunt out of the clubhouse to the parking lot. I look up at the monitor above the bar and watch as they get into the car. Rap stops them as they pull up to the gate and motions Smokey over. Once Smokey gets to them, he helps Rap out of his wheelchair and into the car, and then Smokey takes over gate watch. This is the biggest mistake Smokey has ever made.

"Dad, I don't have a good feeling about any of this." Tea's voice trembles.

ZZ shakes his head, throws his hands into his hair, and howls loudly as he storms out of the clubhouse, leaving me alone with a hurt Tatiana.

It kills me to see her like this. Her brother chose Sabine over his twin sister and his dad. Granted, he hasn't been here long, but still, we always, always stick with family, and I imagine that is exactly what is going through her head as sadness takes over her face.

"My gut is twisting," she says in a soft, broken voice.

My mouth opens, but nothing comes out as I watch her walk away. Dread fills me as her words replay themselves in my head. My eyes go back to the monitor to watch her make it

ZZ

Fucking processing all the bullshit our family is going through right now is more than a goddamn migraine.

Storm and I lost our baby because of those fucking idiots that chased her car, and when my mind thinks about what my Prez and our first lady are going through, it stabs me right in the fucking heart all over again.

When Tatiana finds me, worry glazes her eyes. I know Shadow must have told her I have some news about the pregnancy.

"She's on bed rest for the rest of the pregnancy. She will spend a few more days in the hospital before they allow her to finish it here. She has what they call placenta previa." I explain before she has a chance to ask. "She's going through all this bullshit because of the scarring on her cervix and uterus."

My daughter gasps. "The rape." I say nothing because there is no reason. Her assumption is correct. "But how did the rape affect her uterus?"

I pour a shot as I answer her. "The rape didn't hurt her uterus, but since both are somehow scarred, she ended up with this previa shit. I don't need to ask you to stay on the compound and out of trouble right now, do I? Pyro, Sniper, and I are going to need to be at our best, because fuck no is our Prez gonna be able to handle all this shit while he is worrying. And you know that if I'm worrying about you, I'm not at my best."

"Dad, I'll do my best to stay on the compound, and if I need to leave, I'll take one of the guys with me. I promise."

I toss the shot back and slam the glass down on the table.

"Thanks, baby girl. Your damn brother's got me worried enough. Don't need to be worrying about you, too." My son's fucking with Sabine has my nerves on edge. The bitch is a princess from hell. She's over here to avoid a scandal, so what does that say about her character?

"Dad…"

Fuck. She wants something. "Yeah?" I close my eyes, expecting something much worse than what she brings up.

"Me and Shadow… uh… can—"

Oh, thank fuck. I was thinking she was pregnant, or hell, I don't know what I thought she was going to say, but this is a much better kind of shock.

"It's fine, Tea baby. With the way you've been acting about all this kink shit, and worrying the living shit out of me… It's a breath of fresh air knowin' you two are gonna try. And to be honest with ya, I hope the shit works out, because I know the kid."

I'm actually pleading deep inside for these two to get their shit together. I can't handle having another fucking prick hurt my daughter like before when she was off learning this shit on her own.

"You're serious, aren't you?" she says in disbelief and I chuckle.

"I am."

Tatiana hugs me, kisses me on the cheek, and thanks me before she leaves with a sad smile on her face.

I eased some of her concern, but not all of it. We still have to worry about Winter and her pregnancy and all the other shit.

Now I have to go find my lady because she isn't going to work tonight.

***

Winter

"I can't talk about this!" I scream at my husband. My hands shake as I lay in this hospital bed, knowing that even walking more than twenty feet will put my unborn child at risk. That is how serious my case of placenta previa is.

Braxxon wants me to talk about my feelings and what we need to do about our situation. There isn't anything to discuss. It is what it is. I'm on bed rest for the rest of my pregnancy. The next four and half months will be difficult. Our child's life depends on my following instructions to the letter. And he has forced me to break one of the items on the list by stressing me out and making me yell at him.

"Angel—"

I hold up one of my shaky hands to halt his pleading. "Stop, Braxx. We have enough to worry about, and even the smallest of stresses can end this." I finish with a whisper.

With a huff, my husband sits down on the doctor's rolling chair. I understand that he is frustrated, angry, and a whole lot of other emotions. I am experiencing the exact same thing.

I'm beyond angry. I am enraged, but all that isn't going to help my situation any.

"I'm thirty-one-years old, Angel, and most days, it's as if I'm in my fifties."

Listening to my big bad husband break down in a hushed, exhausted whisper is like a knife to the heart.

Not only do we have this to worry about, we have the Russians, Alec, and any other club shit that comes up. It is always one thing after another, and we can't catch a break.

"Do you want to stay at the live-in, or would you like to rest at home? I could post guards at the house."

I grin at Braxx for the first time in over twenty-four hours, and that is a lot of time to pass without smiling at my husband.

"The live-in is fine. That way I won't stress by seeing guards, and you won't stress leaving me at home when you have club business."

He drops his head and shakes it back and forth. "I'm tired, baby."

A whimper escapes my lips at his announcement. For Braxx to admit he is defeated out loud is not something to be taken lightly.

"Come here." I pat the small hospital bed.

He stands, takes off his wallet chain, and sets it on the tray beside me. When his boots drop to the floor, he climbs into bed with me. I press my forehead against his as his head hits the pillow beside mine. I look into his eyes as I softly speak my next words. "I think you're stressed because, not only do you have all your brothers to protect, you have all the girls, and you have your family with me, too."

His right hand comes up to my cheek and cups it. "Are you scared?"

That's the million dollar question. "I am, but by being with you, and going through everything I have in my life, I know when things are beyond my control. This is one of those things, babe. All I can do... all we can do, is follow the instructions we have been given."

His other hand moves to rest on the small swell of my stomach, his thumb brushing back and forth across it.

"The salons are going to have to wait, Angel—"

I silence him with my lips. It's a small peck, but it is enough for him to know that I understand. We have too much stress to be worrying about opening other businesses at the moment. On the bright side, I'll be on bed rest for the rest of my pregnancy. I can use that time to plan, design, and do something creative and not stressful. It'll be my own personal outlet.

He sighs and shuts his eyes. "I love you."

God, those words coming from him always melt my heart. "I love you, too."

***

Chapter Twenty-One

Shadow

Alec didn't heed our Prez's advice, of course, so Smokey, Sniper, Pyro, and I stand outside of Euphoria mere days later. Due to the Prez stressing over Winter and the baby, the lucky fucker even got a couple extra days. We couldn't give him any longer because we have a point to prove.

"How many guards inside?" Sniper asks, as he climbs off of his lady, drags his rifle out of his side bag, and puts it together.

That motherfucker is scary as shit. I mean, he carries a rifle in pieces on his bike, for fucks sake.

"It's not open right now, so two," I answer as I take the safety off of my gun.

"Can we even get in?" Smokey asks.

I dig the keys to the club out of my pocket. "I pay for a room here, so I have complete access. It may be closed, but there are always a few guards."

Having keys to the building is an advantage of paying for a separate room. The only part we can't access when the building is closed is the dungeon, but I never use it, so I don't give a shit.

"Sniper, seriously, be on watch, man. We got these Russians that we ain't never seen until the other day. Who knows if that was all of them?" Pyro states.

We walk up to the door, and when I open it, we see the first guard. He looks down at my right wrist and then back at me.

174

He recognizes the brothers and me immediately and backs away, not wanting to take part in what is about to happen. The doorman eyes the guns, and instead of following us inside, he leaves. Sniper sneers that he was a smart man as we walk through the corridor of the building in long strides.

I unsnap the clasp on my side knife holster. If circumstances deem it necessary, I will use all the force I have.

We spot the Russians and Alec drinking shots at the bar. None of them senses us as we move to take quick action. We break apart, and when we stand behind them, all at the same time, we cock our guns. Their glasses halt when they hear the sound everyone hates to hear. The cocking is enough to make any man piss himself with cowardice.

"Now, Alec, did you think our Prez was playin' around when he gave you that flawless, serious ultimatum?" I growl as I press the barrel into the base of his neck and his back stiffens.

"Are you fucking kidding me? You're going to come into my club and put a barrel to the back of my neck like a fucking pussy!"

Pyro chuckles as he presses his gun into the Russian he has on point.

With one hand holding my gun in place, I drag my knife out, and with as much force as I can muster with my left hand, I slam it into his hand that rests on the bar top. The bones in his hand crush as my knife nails it into the wood of the counter. His scream is one a chick would be proud of, and we laugh at the scared little pussy.

"You were the one that thought you'd get reinforcement from the Russians. You dumb fuck, you didn't even bring enough of them. If you want to come close to being even with us in a war, you'd better get more than these three little bitches!" I hiss as I move the barrel of my gun away from his neck. I nod to Pyro who is beside me to watch him as I move around the bar.

Once I am in front of Alec, I point my gun between his eyes.

The Russians speak to each other in their own language. We don't give a shit what they say, only that they understand our goddamn point.

"You and your little bitches have until tomorrow to clear the fuck out. This ain't a joke anymore. This club is no longer yours. It is ours. If you want anything you have here, you best get it before the clock hits nine pm. We'll be back by then."

Alec uses his free hand to move the knife sticking out of his other, and my mouth tilts up in that smartass smile that I do best.

"Hurts like a bitch, right? Well think, tomorrow you'll suffer far greater than this if you don't get your ass out of here by the cutoff time. We're done playin' nice. The time for that is over. That man right there," I tip my head towards Pyro, "is our VP, and he has permission to splatter your blood if you don't listen to your last and final warning."

Out of the corner of my eye, I see Feather in the corner, shaking in fear. *Shit.*

"Feather, come," I order her, my voice loud, my words demanding.

She hesitates only for a moment, and then walks towards me on very shaky legs.

"What are you doin' here, darlin'?" I ask, as I tug her closely to my side. She is leaving with me so that Alec doesn't hurt her to get back at me.

When she realizes she is safe at my side, she answers with a quiet tone. "The club is opening soon, and the guard wasn't at the front door, so I walked in and saw this."

Shit. I look down at my watch. No wonder she is here. People will start coming in any minute.

"We gotta wrap this up, brother," Pyro growls, "but first, we need to prove something to this fucker. Darlin', close those beautiful eyes," he says to Feather.

I peer down at her to make sure she has followed my VP's command, and give him a flick of my head to let him know.

The explosive clamor of Pyro's SWAT-K Mini submachine gun fire reverberates through the club as the bullet rips into the nose of one of the Russians. His brains disperse all over the floor behind his slumped body.

The other two recoil in an uproar, and Sniper and Smokey wedge their guns further into the Russians' bodies to stop them from pulling weapons on us.

"So, you see here, Alec, we're not fuckin' playin' around anymore," I growl as I press my pistol to his forehead and squeeze Feather closer into me. I don't want her in harm's way because of us. "This isn't a goddamn game, man. Give this shit up, and go somewhere else to start a new club before you lose your chance."

I will not be able to keep the club from killing him if he doesn't leave. I'll even be the one to pull the trigger because he has pissed me off. We have given him all the chances he is going to get.

"Why the fuck do you even want my club?" Alec tries to yell, but I press my Glock against his throat so it muffles the sound.

How could he be so fucking clueless?

"You aren't taking care of it. You let an unexperienced Sadist harm one of the brother's daughters, you idiot. And you aren't screening motherfuckers properly."

I don't even know why I'm giving him a response. He doesn't deserve one. He lost that right when he didn't take our warning.

"You're still buggin' about that, man! Seriously," he cries.

I lean towards him and yank my knife out of his hand. He cries out again as I drag it up his arm, slicing deep into the muscle. I would shoot him if we weren't trying to be nice and giving him until tomorrow. This will have to do.

"What the fuck is wrong with you!" he screams, and Sniper sighs and smacks his gun upside Alec's head. It knocks him out cold.

"I was tired of his excessive whining. How the fuck you were even friends with that, I'll never know," Sniper says.

I question myself on that, too. This guy is a wimpy ass little shithead.

"Feather, we got these guys under control." I motion to the two guys left. "Go and get me some tape out of the maintenance room. I know there's some in there."

She pulls away, backs up, turns around, and then flees.

"You tapped that, didn't ya?" Smokey chuckles.

My lips tilt up to the side to reveal my answer. The thought of Tatiana finding out how many times I have slept with this girl makes me cringe.

"Here you go," Feather says in a small voice as she comes up and hands me the duct tape.

"Thank you, babe," Pyro says.

I'm too busy thinking of the guilt churning in my stomach. I wonder why that is though. I have nothing to be ashamed of. We haven't committed to one another, and now, that thought repeats itself over in my head and is the only thing I can think.

"Sorry," I mumble as Sniper takes the roll to tape up the guy. He has to be tired of holding his gun on him, and here I am all spaced out.

After they are secured, and we're satisfied with the way we're leaving things here, we trudge outside to our bikes.

"You got anywhere to stay for a few weeks?" our VP asks Feather as we straddle the seats of our ladies.

"I do. I'll go to my sister's. Shadow, you have my number. Call when it's safe for me to come home, please."

I reach up and tuck a strand of hair behind her ear. "I will, darlin'. No worries."

We watch as she walks to her car. We don't start our bikes until she safely pulls out of the lot.

***

Chapter Twenty-Two

Shadow

When we get back to the compound, our Prez doesn't even give us a second to calm down before he calls us into the chapel. It isn't a meeting. It's a follow up to what happened. Piper takes all of our guns and puts them in the safe before we can enter and sit down.

Pyro lights a joint, takes a few hits, and passes it around the table as our Prez takes a seat.

"So what happened?"

Pyro, being VP, goes on about what went down and what we should expect.

"He really didn't think we were fuckin' serious?" Prez asks in disbelief.

I puff on the joint before I pass it along. "Nope. He was in shock that we're still pissed off about what happened to Tatiana."

Prez grumbles under his breath before speaking. "Well fuck, I wanted no blood shed. Winter can lose the baby if we don't keep the stress level down. And she is set on staying here until the pregnancy is over."

Well, that complicates things. We need to keep the blood away from the compound, and the club is where we have the high ground. We can only hope we will be able to hit him at Euphoria tomorrow night before he hits us here. That is, if he has the balls to do that in the first place.

"Thanks, brothers. Go do your thing. I got a wife to attend to. Be well rested for tomorrow. I don't need any sleep deprived motherfuckers when we hit him hard."

We stand at the same time and let the Prez leave before we follow suit. I already know where I am going.

Tatiana. She is the only thing that crosses my mind tonight. I am finished thinking about all this other bullshit, and what better way to disconnect myself from it all than to bury myself deep inside of her and forget everything.

I walk through the clubhouse, out to the parking lot, and into the live-in building. I let the door slam shut behind me and walk towards the stairs. I don't dare stop to greet anyone lingering around. I am done with pleasantries and threats. My demons and I are going to forget for a while.

***

I knock on her door. I don't wait for her to answer, but I do give her the courtesy of knowing someone is about to enter. When I shut the door behind me, I stand there and watch her. She is lying on her stomach, earbuds in as her foot bounces up and down to whatever she's listening to. She looks at peace, carefree even. I decide I'll wait until morning to tell her everything that is going down tomorrow.

Before I came to her room, I did stop at mine to grab my new pinwheel. I have been itching to use one on her ever since I fucked her tight little asshole.

I want to drag it across her body, prick, and scratch at her skin until it almost bleeds. I want to tear the first layer of that beautiful, flawless, tanned, toned body until she screams for me to stop.

181

So, I do what I have been craving to do. I take the pinwheel, press it against her foot, and drag it up her leg. She pulls the earbuds out of her ears, lets out a screech, and her body flies around.

"SHADOW!"

I chuckle at her, bring a finger to my mouth, and shush her quiet. She obeys and lays down on her back.

"We aren't going to do a scene, but I'm going to provide pain and pleasure," I growl while I drag the wheel up her leg and tease the apex of her thighs. "I'm going to make your skin sore before I fuck your pussy raw."

Tatiana bites her lip so hard that when her teeth free that plump juiciness, the pressure she applied leaves a strong crimson color in its wake.

"Nervous?" I laugh as I press the wheel hard against her center, and she whispers no.

"Good, because tonight, I don't want you scared."

Tatiana has a long way to go before I can truly scene with her. I'll be patient because she shows genuine interest in learning the lifestyle. She handled me exceptionally well the first time.

"We're going to take this slow. Not this," I tease, indicating tonight, "but us, learning one another. I'm a confusing person, babe. I don't do the slave/submissive type of shit. I'm a Dom who loves to top. It's as easy as that. I don't do switches, so if you ever try to control me, it'll end with you tied up and at my mercy."

As the words come out of my mouth, I almost want to challenge her to do that. I love having her tied up. It is such a beautiful sight. She makes a good little bottom.

"You're serious." She beams at me.

"I am." I run the pinwheel up to her tits and circle her nipples lightly as I answer her. If this has any chance of working, I will have to accept and commit to the patience of teaching her. I've never taken on a commitment as strong as this one. I'm looking forward to it, nonetheless.

"So… you and me?"

Never in my life have I heard those words and thought they'd sound as enchanting as they do coming from her lips.

Mmmmm is the only response I can give her while I'm in this state. Her nipples turn a beautiful wine color as I roll the wheel back and forth, not cutting the skin, but aggravating it. My demons want me to drag it deeper, slice the skin, and I am holding back, that is…

"Whatcha doin, darlin'," I hum when one of her hands touches the wrist wielding the pinwheel.

"You can press down. Your eyes are the blackest I've ever seen them, and I know you're itching to draw my blood."

I throw my head back and groan before I bring it back down to glimpse at her. She is genuine, I sense it.

I flick my wrist back and forth, edge the wheel deep enough to peel the first small layer of skin back. She doesn't scream or even make a peep as I continue to roll it back and forth.

"It is indescribable," she sighs in the softest voice.

Occasions such as this are the only times I regret not being able to go regular vanilla. I long for the day I won't require the things I do to get off. Tatiana is exquisite with her hair spread, and her blue, innocent doe eyes staring at me. She deserves the world.

183

Her skin trickles a drop of blood, and that is all it takes for my cock to harden in my jeans. I toss the pinwheel to the floor and peel myself free of the constricting fabric. I don't bother undressing. I'm hard enough to fuck her.

"Wiggle them bottoms that you call shorts off right fuckin now!"

Tatiana gives me a devious grin before she complies. She moves quick. Maybe she is experiencing the same urgency I am.

"Can you at least pull my hair hard as you fuck me?"

Oh, fuck yes! "Flip over, darlin', I'm gonna fuck that pussy doggy style." I'll pull those blonde curls so fucking hard her scalp will scream crimson.

Her pert little ass is in the air in less than ten seconds. It begs me to slap at it, so I bring my palm up and land a huge blow to her right cheek and she moans. It is such a delicate sound.

"Once more," I growl, and she moans yes.

This time I bring my hand up and slap with all the force my arm will allow. My cock can no longer stay away. I climb up on the bed, press my right hand into her lower back to make her arch deeper, and with my left hand, I position my cock against her wet folds. I close my eyes to take it all in. Tatiana is something to treasure, and each time my cock is lucky enough to enter any part of her body, I plan to savor it as my last.

"Shadow," she whimpers.

I chuckle and ram into her.

Her pussy automatically responds to my cock, squeezing it tightly as her juices coat me. Even fucking her astonishes me. She flips her head further back to remind me she wants that sexy-as-fuck hair pulled. I move my right hand into her tresses, and with a solid yank, I jerk it back.

"SHIT!" she screams.

I shift my left hand to her hip and pound into her with no mercy. Her cries make my balls tighten. The red of her scalp shows me she is in pain, and only furthers the assault my cock is delivering her.

Each of my pounds inside of her is met with a thrust right back at me. She manages to keep pace with me even as I snap her head back and use her locks to deepen my thrusts.

"Can I come, please?" she pants.

My palm lands on her ass. "Yes," I hiss through gritted teeth as my balls tighten with such fire, they ache. "Now," I shout, pounding into her.

When I release and her body slumps to the bed, I pull out and collapse beside her. I'm fucking spent after such a long day.

"That's the most basic sex I've fuckin had since I was a teenager." I chuckle. It wasn't technically straight vanilla, but close enough I'm shocked.

"Yeah, well, I'm stripping down and going to sleep. I'm tired." She yawns.

Who knew a quick fuck could exhaust a person. I haven't had sex that fast in a long ass time.

"I'll be here when you wake," I say, stripping my clothes off at the same time.

"We'll see," she says sleepily. "Night."

I gaze at her as she strips herself free from her clothes, tucks herself under the sheet, and her eyes close.

"Night, darlin'," I whisper.

***

Chapter Twenty-Three

Tatiana

The heat of the sun beats down onto my bare back as I wake from my sex-induced coma. My mouth splits into a smile because Shadow is rubbing my thigh. I inwardly squeal. I can't believe last night happened, and I'm more than happy that he slept in my bed again. This time is a lot different. He made it clear there would be no repeat performance of the morning after our first time.

"Good mornin, darlin'," he drawls. "I know you're awake."

I turn my head to look at him. His deep onyx eyes sparkle, and he rubs my back with a slow torturous pace that lights me ablaze.

"Morning. Did you sleep okay?" I ask him. I hope he did. He appears well rested.

"I did, but I promised myself I would tell you what is going on as soon as we woke up. You deserve to know things, darlin', and I don't know if anyone will tell you or not. And after this," he gestures between us, "I'm obligated to tell you shit. It wouldn't be right if I didn't."

Why does this make me queasy? As I sit up, I drag the white sheet with me to cover my chest and then give him my full attention.

"Go ahead, tell me whatever it is."

He flops onto his back and peers up at the ceiling. He is

pensive, that is certain, and it worries me.

"You can't leave the compound at all today. Promise that you won't."

I reach over, grab his cheek, and turn his face towards mine. "Why?" I ask. I have to be able to see into his eyes when he answers me.

"We got business at Euphoria. It'll get dirty. Stay here. Do. Not. Leave. We don't want to worry about anybody while we're there. Let me rephrase that. We don't need something new to worry about."

I fling my head back against the headboard, groan, and shout out as the pain shoots through my skull. I shouldn't have thrown my head so hard. Now I am going to have a splitting damn headache all day, on top of all this other bullshit.

"It is always something, isn't it?" I whisper more to myself than to him.

"Here lately it's always something, and it pisses me off as much as it pisses you off."

I know that I have to promise to stay on the compound. I won't worry my family or Shadow while they have other business to attend. I want to hear more about him and for him to keep talking to me so openly.

"What's your name?" I tease him to lighten the mood.

His eyes light up as he sits up to lean on the headboard. "It's Tavis, Tea."

My smile tilts to a frown because he didn't tell me the truth. "Okay, you don't have to tell me," I say, disappointed.

Shadow grabs my hand in his and puts our joint clasped hands into his lap. "It is, darlin', I swear."

But if his name is Tavis, why does he use it as a scene name? This confuses me. I don't really understand the reasoning behind doing that. Everything I have read says not to use your real name if you aren't with a permanent partner. This goes to show me, I should never, ever use the internet as my only source.

"Wipe that nasty face away. I use my real name to scene because, unlike everyone else, I don't have a life to hide from, or a job that I could lose if it becomes known I'm a Sadist. A lot of others are worried about jail time, losing their jobs, or their family finding out. Look around, baby." Shadow grins. "Do I have anyone here that doesn't support me? Do I have a family that would frown at my life choices? Do I have a job that requires my personal life to be kept quiet? No, I don't have any of those things. Everyone here supports me, and my job is of the flexible variety." He winks at me. "I have it a lot easier than most kinksters do."

Well, all this makes sense, and the name, in a fucked up way, fits him, but I could never call him Tavis on a personal level. He is Shadow to me. If he wants me to call him Tavis while we're in bed together, I'll do it, but I can't do it all the time. I don't care how well that name suits him, he will always be Shadow to me.

"I didn't expect that, to be honest with you. I thought it would be something horribly awful like Bobby Lou or something funky like that," I smirk as I play with him.

"Bobby Lou? Really? Is there anyone with that name?" He chuckles, and I grab my phone off the nightstand to Google the name.

"Let's find out, shall we?" I giggle as I type in the silly name, but as I repeat it, it doesn't sound all that silly. "Wow! It's a really common name, believe it or not," I say as I hand him my phone so he can see. I can't believe it really is that popular of a name, and the more I sound it out with my lips, the more it grows on me. Go figure.

"It sounds appealing now, doesn't it?" he replies as he hands me my phone. "All joking aside, you're going to promise to stay on the compound today, right? Because, darlin', I can't worry about you while I'm working, and ZZ sure the fuck doesn't need to worry either. Please listen to all of us for once. Do as you're told. I know that's the last thing that you want to hear, and it's the last thing I would ever want to ask you. I wouldn't be practically begging on my knees for you to stay home where you will be safe."

When his tone takes on a strange high pitch with his last sentence, it pulls at me in the weirdest way. "Are you okay?"

I'm concerned, very damn concerned. For Shadow to show any kind of insecurities, more than freaks me out. Why are the guys suddenly showing me new sides to them? I don't enjoy being thrown for a million and one loops. It stresses me out.

"I am, Tea, now that we've done this." He gestures between us again. "It's serious. This thing between us is fucking serious as shit. I wouldn't risk hurting you with all my bullshit if it wasn't. You were there. You know exactly how much I tried to resist us getting together."

No shit, there were so many weird, awkward moments where we both pulled at one another and fought constantly, until the other day. This is definitely a step in the other direction for us. It happened fast, too.

"Shadow, is this your messed up way of telling me we're exclusive, and you'll be hurt if something happens to me?"

190

I'm not making light of the conversation this time. I'm completely serious. He is acting like it will rip him to shreds if I get hurt.

"Darlin', we've been exclusive ever since I fucked your ass bare."

The little fuckwad. "Way to a girl's heart, Shadow," I grumble as I go to stand.

"Tea, stop. You know I was being serious before I went all horny idiot on you."

It still sucks that he worded it that way, but then I remember who he is, and what he does for a living, and who our family is. These men aren't filtered, and god forbid someone ever try to muzzle them like they deserve most of the time.

"I know. Oh, and I'll stay here today. I won't leave the compound, but please keep an eye on my brother. That bitch has her claws so far deep in him, I ain't sure he has balls anymore. He's a pussy whipped bastard because of Sabine."

When I mention her name, he cringes beside me. Yeah, I don't like hearing it nor saying it, either.

"Has he been back at all?" he asks, breaking me from my evil thoughts of Winter's sister.

"Yeah, but he isn't speaking to anyone. I've only known him for a few months. This isn't like him. I don't know what else to say."

I'm disappointed in my brother. For him to go against our father's wishes is a big deal, and it makes it even worse that he is trying to patch in. He isn't listening to a patched member. He has repeatedly messed up. I wish I knew what was going through his head. Mace has only wanted to please his newly

191

found family. This goes against all things Breakneck when you're patching in. I only worry that this will affect their decisions to let him continue to prospect.

"Your dad isn't happy, Tea. He's voiced that."

"I know." I scoot down on the bed so that my head hits the soft pillows.

Shadow moves closer to me. "This shit is depressing as fuck," he growls as he tickles me. "Were you the one watchin' me?"

Ah, hell. "A few times I did." I gasp as he continues to tickle torture me. "I do believe you were watching me as well."

"You little shit," he murmurs as he moves on top of me. "I thought I was losin' my edge, darlin'."

Never.

He stops tickling me and gazes down, his face taking on an entirely new expression. "You're really pretty, Tea."

Heart failure. I try to turn my head, but he reaches up to grasp my cheeks. "No, I'm serious. You're beautiful. You're a natural blonde. You hardly wear makeup, and by some fuckin' weird, wacky female shit, you're toned, and you don't even work out. Women are jealous of you. That I know for sure."

I stop trying to move his hands from my cheeks, and let my blue eyes stare into the depths of his. They speak to me that he is sincere. He really finds me attractive, and I'm perfect in his eyes, even though I know that I am far from being perfect. "Thank you," I say through my squeezed cheeks and lips.

He chuckles. "Get dressed. I'm fuckin starved!"

***

Chapter Twenty-Four

Shadow

I know I'm not the only one who is worried about leaving the women. Things seem to go sideways every time we leave. It isn't until we pull into the parking lot of Euphoria and see it closed that relief flows through me. He didn't open it, so I know he is in there, waiting on us. We knew he wouldn't be bold enough to do this where cameras could pick up on all the things that are about to happen. Pulling into the lot is a loud, drastic move on our part, and we don't give a flying fuck. All the brothers want this shit over and done with.

Each time we are close to a little bit of peace and freedom, it is yanked from our grasps. We haven't had half a year where we could relax, settle down, and enjoy life. It is exhausting, and I would love to be able to work on engines, smoke, fuck, and sleep, but since I came to the Master Charter, I haven't been able to do any of those things.

I pull my illegal Mini Uzi out of my saddlebag as my brothers pull massive machinery out of theirs. With quiet steps, we edge ourselves through the parking lot and against the wall of the building. Sniper guards our Prez, and I hold the door open while Pyro moves the barrel of one of his guns through the threshold. Once Smokey has a good grip on the large metal door, Pyro, ZZ, and I ease in. When the hall is clear, I give the signal to Smokey, and he relays one to Sniper and the Prez. It is so quiet you could hear a pin drop, and it automatically puts us in fight or flight mode.

Pyro rounds the corner and ducks behind a side wall, and we all very slowly follow suit. Pyro peeks around the wall, and flicks his fingers for me to move to the one across from us.

I crotch down and move quickly to the other side and motion for Smokey to follow. I'm about to say this was too easy. There is no fucking way in hell we can get away with coming in here and them not knowing, but then a bullet hits the wall next to Smokey.

"Why can't you assholes talk shit out!" Alec's loud voice booms out through the echo of the bullet. "This could have been fucking solved by now, but no, you want it all. You motherfuckers want goddamn everything!"

The Prez tries to slip from the safety of Sniper who is quick to jerk him back against the protection of the wall. "Don't move," Sniper growls at his brother.

"We tried to talk it out. We did. You could've made out like a bandit and took the money I offered and started up somewhere other than my fuckin' town!" Prez tosses back.

"Which is the stupidest thing you could've offered me. Why the fuck would I have started a club here if I wanted to up and move two years later?"

This is going to take a long ass while.

Light comes from the hallway where the entrance door is, and I swing my gun in that direction. *Shit!* If he called for more backup, we are fucking cornered, and there is nowhere else to go. But it is much worse than that as I see two blonde heads come into view.

Mace Jr. and Sabine.

"Get the fuck down!" I roar as I reach for Sabine who, by my fucked up luck, is closer to me than Mace Jr. is.

Fire rings out, and our worst fear comes to life. The takeover has gone wrong. A bullet rips through Mace Jr.'s neck. His legs give out, and he tumbles backwards as ZZ rips from the wall, screaming at the top of his lungs.

"Take off your goddamn shirt and press it to his wound, you stupid bitch," ZZ roars at Sabine when she comes to from the shock and does as he instructs.

"Them fuckers are dead!" ZZ thunders, murder rippling in his voice.

There is no next move as we all head straight into rapid fire, ducking behind everything we can. I end up behind the bar and can't see any of my brothers. I can only see flying bullets and fire coming out of barrels when I jerk up and take blind shots.

When the gunfire slows, I wait a few moments before I peek out, and a bullet flies beside my head, shattering a bottle on the shelf behind me.

"Goddamn it!" I roar as I stand and aim at the Russian who almost killed my ass. "You better kill me before I blow your goddamn brains out!"

I don't pull my finger away from the trigger, and bullets ping from my UZI and into his body, one right after another. His large frame falls to the floor. I duck back behind the bar, take an extra magazine out of my pocket, and let the empty one fall to the floor as I slide the new one in place.

"Head count," Pyro yells. "Prez?"

Our Prez shouts he's good.

"Sniper?"

He shouts he's fucking peachy.

"Shadow?"

"I'm fucking still intact," I holler.

"Smokey?"

A few seconds go by before he answers in a pained voice. "Took one to the fuckin' shoulder."

"ZZ," Pyro calls.

"I'm fucking here and my son is fucking dead!"

Fuck, this shit has just moved to an entirely new level.

"You bastards killed my brother's fucking kid. You're all going to hell," Prez howls right before guns start roaring again.

I'm finished with ducking behind this bar like a fucking pussy. This shit just got real, and I am about to kill me some fucking assholes! I take out my pistol and grip it with my left hand while I stand, firing rapidly at anything that moves and isn't one of my brothers. Thank fuck for the leather cuts. My eyes see nothing but red and orange flashes, and my ears hear nothing but the explosion of bullets hitting all around me.

The gunfire comes to halt when one last person is left standing on the opposing side.

Alec.

Go fucking figure his luck.

"ZZ, he's yours," Prez grits through his locked teeth. "Torture his sorry ass!"

I know just the place to take him so ZZ can unleash all his fury.

197

The dungeon.

"Grab a hold of him and follow me," I say as I cough to clear my scratchy throat from the gun smoke and yelling.

My ears ring with echoes of the gunshots that linger inside of my head as we make our way to the dungeon. It isn't a real dungeon, but it's this club's version of one. We ignore Alec's cries of protests as I fling open the door and gesture them in with one hand. If they can't figure out what to do with all the shit in here, then my brothers have no business torturing fuckers.

"Well, lookie there." Sniper chuckles deviously at the sight of shackles hanging from the ceiling. "Chain him up so our brother can get his torch on."

A smile lights my face and I grab one of Alec's arms as the Prez grabs the other. We have him immobilized in less than a minute.

ZZ unclips a big ass knife from the holster on his hip and growls, "I ain't playing games with this fucking piece of shit. I'm skinning him, and we're gonna burn this fucking club to the ground with his ass still alive. I want him to feel the heat on his open flesh."

If it weren't such a good idea, I'd speak up about losing a perfectly good club, but this way, it will look like a kink accident gone wrong, while gangsters took a go at one another upstairs. Less cleanup for us is always a good thing.

A few things plague my mind. "Why the fuck were the Russians here, Alec?"

He doesn't answer until ZZ holds his knife up to his throat, digs it into his flesh, and growls for him to answer my question.

"Fuck, okay." He sputters. "I picked some random Russian strangers and paid them for protection." He coughs and continues. "I apparently chose the wrong ones."

"Yeah, no shit. Look where you are now, motherfucker. Poor intimidation tactics. Your assuming that we're afraid of our enemies is the biggest mistake you made. Now, it will cost you your life." *Wait.* "Where the fuck is Sabine?" I ask while I move away from Alec.

Smokey gestures behind him. "Thought she should see who the fuck she's messing with. Bitch got her ass shot in the line of fire, too." He hoots loudly.

The sound that comes from my mouth is anything but a sane one. The bitch fucking deserves the wound.

Alec's whimpers grate on my nerves while we wait for ZZ to strip the flesh from his bones. This is going to be one nasty as hell torture session. ZZ keeps his leather gloves on and bitches that he's about to ruin them. Chuckles light up the room, and they are anything but friendly.

"I think I'll start with his back," he murmurs while he cuts off Alec's shirt.

I hold up my hand for ZZ to halt as I search for a ballgag. No way in hell can I take the excessive screaming for a minute longer. When I find a dirty one sitting on a shelf, it only lights my fury towards Alec. Fucking dumbass was slacking so bad.

"Use this germ infested fucker," I growl as I toss it to ZZ.

He catches it, forces it into Alec's mouth, and buckles the snaps in the back. "Look at that. We muffled the dog."

ZZ cranks his neck side to side before he scrapes his long blade down half of Alec's back. Alec's eyes widen as a scream chokes its way through the gag. Blood pours as ZZ peels his flesh straight down to the bone. Sabine screams that we're killing him, and I am surprised our Prez doesn't slap her. When ZZ removes the second ribbon of muscle on the back, Alec passes out.

"What a little pansy ass." I snort. "He can dish out pain, but the motherfucker sure as shit can't take it."

"Can two of you put my son in that bitch's car? I'll only be a little longer. It's no fun when they pass out."

Smokey grabs Sabine by the arm, yanks her up, and follows Sniper out of the dungeon.

I throw my head back and roar with laughter. My fucked up demons laugh along with me as ZZ moves to Alec's front and begins to cut him there.

Alec's eyes fly open for a split second before he passes right back out.

"Jesus fuck! Really?" ZZ laughs while he knives his way down through the cartilage and muscle.

That is one fucking, disgusting ass sight.

"Brother, that shit is fucked up," I joke. My shoulders heave as nausea hits me, and I push the urge to upchuck away.

"No shit," Prez retorts. His shoulders follow suit of mine. "Smokey sent a text. They're takin' your son back to the compound," he informs us.

When ZZ hears the Prez, he lets out an animalistic roar and tears the last bit of flesh off Alec's chest.

"I'm done. Let's get the hell out of here," he says while he cleans his knife on his pants.

"Pyro, do your thing, brother," Prez tells him as we walk out of the dungeon, through the ruined club, and into the parking lot.

It's time for damage control because I know my girl is going to be fucked up in the head over her brother's death. I don't wait for the rest of them. I can't. Tatiana is going to be so tore up over this, who knows how the hell she will handle it.

***

Chapter Twenty-Five

Breakneck Chapter

Aftermath

Winter

I glare at my sister as Doc patches up her gunshot wound. She whines from the pain, and I want to slap the shit out of her, but I can't because I'm lying down in bed, angry that I can't get up. She is the last person that should be allowed to cry. She got Mace Jr. killed. Her claws were sunk so far deep in him, he couldn't see past her beauty, and it cost him his life.

My hands shake with so much anger as I dial my mother on my cell. It goes straight to her voicemail, and without hesitation, I leave the nastiest message I have ever left a human being before.

"It's Winter. You have one day to come and get your cunt of a daughter, or I'll let the tabloids know everything there is to know about her slutty behavior!" I hiss into the receiver before hanging up.

"No reason to be such a bitch!" Sabine growls.

"People are dead because of you!" Unbelievable.

Doc closes his case, mumbles that she'll be fine if she keeps the wound clean, and then walks out of my bedroom without another word. Who's to blame him? He's had to clean up our messes a lot lately. I don't even want to know what is going on downstairs. I'm sure it is filled with hysteria, and ZZ, Tatiana and Berry are more than a mess.

"You had a motive for sleeping with him, and we're going to figure it out. And then you'll be lucky if someone here doesn't hunt your ass down. You walking out of here, still breathing? That's a blessing. After you're gone, don't contact me again. I'm done with you AND our mother."

I reach for the bottle of water on my nightstand, and as it goes down my throat, I wish it was hardcore alcohol. The stress on me is too much, and Braxxon is going to rain fire down on Sabine when he finally makes it up here.

Mace Jr. was a fucking kid. A kid my stupid ass sister got killed because of her obviously addictive crotch. It has to be magical. It put little Mace under a spell that no one could break. He was so set on being accepted here, and then my sister came along and put him under some weird trance.

"He made his own decision to go to the club. I went along for the ride, and I got shot for it!"

Jesus, she thinks we're going to believe that lie?

"Whatever, Sabine. I won't listen to it anymore, but I can't let you leave this room until our mother gets here, because someone down there will most likely kill you if you so much as open your mouth. So sit there, shut the fuck up, and don't fucking piss me off!"

***

Tatiana

I rock back and forth and shudder at the dried blood caked to my arms. I can't clean it up. I can't move. I can't talk. All I can do is replay the image of them carrying my brother into the compound, blood still leaking from the bullet wound in his neck.

I don't understand what happened. I can't even imagine what went down, or why my brother is no longer alive. Everything is a big blur, and everyone shouting about what went wrong isn't helping me.

Funny thing is I don't even want to know. Knowing isn't going to bring him back from the dead. All it will do is scar me more. I am making myself numb. It's the only way I will survive living this life that I was born into.

The first person I lost to a tragic death was my grandfather, and after that, it was a non-stop ride on the train of death. It hasn't stopped chugging. The evil in this world keeps stocking the engine with coal.

What is my dad going to tell his adoptive parents? How *do* you tell parents that their only son is dead?

I can't bear it. I can't. All these emotions swirl inside of me, designing a tapestry of hate.

And Sabine, she's been here a few days, and she had my brother so wrapped up in her, he couldn't see left from right, or good from bad. She is the reason he is dead, I suspect. If I hear that she is the cause, there is no telling what I might do. The anger makes me so hot that my ears heat.

"Tea, baby, you need to clean up," Shadow says quietly as he bends down in front of my shaking body.

He needs to go away. I can't deal with all the extra emotions that emanate from being near him. The atmosphere that radiates is too strong for me to handle as I grieve in my shocked state.

"No, leave me alone." I push him away.

He doesn't listen. Instead, he rests his knees on the carpet in front of me, takes me in his arms, and yanks me into his chest.

"Cry, darlin'. Don't hold it in."

I don't want to cry. I want to sit here and bounce back and forth in peace. Can't he see that? I want to be left the hell alone.

"Please, let go of me," I whisper into his chest. "I need time to myself."

***

Shadow

"Please, let go of me," she whispers into my chest. "I need time to myself."

The plea in her voice is like a knife to the gut. She isn't even crying, and that worries me. Tatiana has always been one to express her feelings. She doesn't keep them bottled in. When her arms break free, she shoves me away, and then kicks off with her rocking.

I stay where I am for a few more seconds and then stand. She

205

isn't going to allow me to comfort her. If she is pushing me away, it speaks a loud message to leave her the fuck alone. I wish I could clean the blood off her at least. She's too beautiful to be covered in gore from her brother. I step back slowly, turn around, and make my way towards the commotion in the kitchen.

"I'm gonna kill that fucking bitch! He was a prospect. He shouldn't have even been there," ZZ yells at the top of his lungs.

Storm and Piper scoot away from him. His face is bright red and the veins pulsate in his forehead. Blood covers the floor, and his dead son lies on the kitchen table. Bloody rags litter the room, but no one dares to pick them up.

"He wasn't even fucking nineteen years old," ZZ shouts as his fist plows through one of the cabinet doors, snapping it right off the hinges.

Prez comes into the room and looks around as he rubs his temples. He is stressed to the maximum.

"Get her the fuck outta here, Prez." ZZ tries to speak more calmly.

No shit. Sabine wanted adventure. Who the fuck says that when guns go off? The stupid bitch.

"Winter made a call to their mom and left a message. If she isn't gone by tomorrow morning, I'll escort her outta town myself," Prez answers ZZ. "Brother, what do you want to do?"

We look from the Prez to ZZ, and then back down to Mace Jr. whose eyes are wide open. Jesus, no one bothered to shut them? I stalk towards him, take two fingers, and close his eyes.

"Have him cremated, and afterwards, I'll take his ashes to the family that raised him," ZZ says. Defeat is written in every line of his body.

***

Chapter Twenty-Six

Tatiana

Last night, I watched as my brother's body was loaded into a hearse, and was taken away from us to be cremated. He won't even get a proper burial because of the way he died. How is that fair to him? He didn't deserve to go out the way he did.

I shut down exactly twelve hours ago. I let my feelings dissipate into thin air. The logical side of my brain screams for me to open up, to let people in. I refuse to listen to it. My brain doesn't experience my emotions. My heart does, and my heart is finished being broken.

The gate opens to allow Winter's mother to waltz in with her guards. As if we don't have enough going on.

"Why do you have these assholes with you?" Godfather laughs as he crosses his arms.

"I never go anywhere without them. I brought them the last time I was here. You should have expected this." Iiana, Winter's mom, answers.

"Take your fuckin' trashy ass daughter, and get the fuck outta my town. My wife is stressed the fuck out." Godfather yells, and before anyone has time to blink, Iiana's men pull their guns.

The brothers waste no time drawing their own, and train them on Iiana's men.

"You send your daughter to my town without askin', and then

you come here and draw on my family. Are you outta your fucking, goddamn mind?" Braxxon roars, his voice vicious and his entire body stiff with anger.

More guns. It is always more guns. There is never any peace here. I am so sick and tired of all this shit being brought to our door. I lost my brother last night, and now I have to worry about someone else I love being shot because of Sabine and her mother?

There comes a time in one's life where she slams into the one wall that blocks her paths, and that person either gives up or knocks it down. I am *not* the person who gives up. I am going to be the bulldozer who plows it down. I'm done being nice. For years, they thought they kept this part of the business locked away from me. My ears were always listening, always paying attention to what was going on. Yeah, I was a spoiled brat, but this spoiled brat knows more than they think I do.

And if Winter's mom thinks she is going to come in here and draw a gun on me, she is mistaken. I am not like most of the club members. If you pull a gun on me, you better intend to kill me.

Shadow jerks my arm to move me behind him, and I shove him while I grab the gun from the back of his pants. When I turn around, I aim it straight at the guy stupid enough to be holding his gun at me. I point at his gut and pull the trigger. I have no clue what kept everyone from opening fire after I did this. Everyone watches the guy fall to the ground with a loud cry as he grips at the bullet wound. My hands are steady, and no remorse flows through my veins.

"Get your bleeding man and your princess, and get the fuck off my property." Braxxon explodes.

My gun remains aimed at the man on the ground. "You don't

point a gun at me unless you plan on using it," I hiss.

My father comes up and gently lowers my arm. "Shh, baby, it's okay," he soothes.

I don't respond as Dad fingers the gun from my grasp. ZZ is not a gentle character, and I'm alert enough to sense the tender, soothing way he uses to care for me. His actions and tone speak of his distress over what transpired a few moments ago. His daughter shot a man, a man who is laying there, bleeding to death, while I have no remorse whatsoever for doing it.

How can I feel bad for shooting this idiot? He was aiming a gun at me. If he were a patched member, he would know he shouldn't have let mine or Shadow's movements confuse him. He should have kept his eyes on my every move, and maybe then, he wouldn't be dripping crimson all over the concrete of the compound.

"They weren't going to shoot you. There was no reason for that." Iiana chuckles.

I want to scream, "Don't you give a shit about anything that is happening?" I shot her man down, and she's over there laughing. Why would they pull their guns out if they didn't plan on using them?

"Ma'am, I think I'm dying," the guy I shot moans.

I roll my eyes. Of course he's dying. I shot him directly in the gut. Who knows what organs I might have hit.

"Darlin'." Shadow pulls me back against his body and keeps his gun trained on the enemies. "Don't you fuckin' move from my side, or so help me," he growls low into my ear.

I try to jerk away. I am through caring about what everyone wants me to do. I'm going to do what I want, when I want, and how I want, from now on. If these assholes can, so can I. Having a vagina doesn't make me inadequate.

"If you jerk me against you one more time, I swear to god," I hiss back.

"Mother, take Sabine and go. We have had enough," Winter says as she walks into the circle outlined with guns. Is she crazy?

"Angel, what the fuck?" Braxxon hollers, while he moves her behind him.

"You're supposed to be on bed rest, Win. Come on," Piper persuades her.

"I'll go, but if they aren't gone in five minutes, I'm calling the cops. I'm done doing this shit the illegal way. If they won't leave, I'll get the cops and the media to do the job." She shoots an evil grin at her mother.

The media is the last thing this place wants to deal with. It might open secrets that need to stay buried deep down in the hard desert ground. We definitely don't want anybody digging that shit up.

"Get back in bed, Angel. You can't be up and moving around!" Braxxon growls.

She retreats backwards and doesn't answer him.

"Get your people and leave," Braxxon repeats.

Iiana orders her men to pick up the guy that I shot. I honestly don't care if he dies or not. That is how disgusted I am that they had the audacity to point a gun in my face, as if I was the one who was spewing threats. Sabine rolls her bags towards the gate, and Rap opens it to reveal the black SUVs that Iiana and her men arrived in.

"Don't come back, and I assure you, Angel won't be contacting you again." Braxx reminds her, "You have until the morning to get the fuck outta my town."

I wouldn't have given her that much time.

"If my daughter wants to create a family with white trash, then she can," Iiana spits out, adding fuel to the already steaming hot fire blazing in the compound.

Oh, why couldn't she leave when she was asked? Why would she run her mouth more, only to feed the already burning situation? People don't learn. She's been ordered to leave, and now she runs her mouth? It's like she loves to push other's buttons so hard that there is no going back.

"OUT!" my dad screams. "Your bitch of a daughter talked my son into going into a mess, and he got fuckin' killed. You're lucky I didn't put a fuckin' bullet into her skull. If you're not out of here in the next thirty seconds, all of your motherfucking brains are gonna be splattered on this cement," he roars, aiming his gun directly at her head.

Shadow's free hand moves to my stomach so that he can get a better handle over me. I stop trying to fight and lean into his body. I don't give a fuck anymore. This is my life, this is what I know, and I have to accept this is how it is always going to be.

***

Shadow

Tatiana has given up. I felt it when she shot that guy in the gut. It was the strangest thing. It was as if all the sweet in her turned sour. She isn't sorry she shot the guy. She knew what she was doing, and she knew what the result would be from the action she chose. All I can do is hold her until these people are gone, because if someone so much as lays a finger on her, I will kill them.

When Rap hits the button to close the gate, everyone lets out a breath. We don't want to lose anyone else. In my opinion, everyone is still in damn shock over Mace Jr.'s death. It was a fast one. He came out of nowhere.

"Tatiana, I'm not sugarcoatin' this shit. You most likely killed that guy," ZZ tells her.

She shrugs against my body before she answers back. "He pointed his gun at me. I'm tired of guns being pointed around here. At least he won't be able to point a gun at another innocent woman."

I chuckle and squeeze her closer to me as I tuck my gun back in the holster. ZZ hands me the one he took from her, and I tuck it back in my waistband. I'll have to dispose of it later. I'll be damned if I take the risk of Winter's mom turning the dead guy over to the cops, and the possibility of the bullet and gun being traced back to Tea.

"Tatiana, go inside. I have to talk with Shadow," ZZ orders her and everyone scatters.

Prez took off as soon as the gate closed, no doubt to bitch at Winter for getting out of bed and risking her and the baby's health.

I watch her retreat inside before I turn back to ZZ. "I can't believe she fuckin' did that," I hiss and let my frustration finally show.

"She's gone cold. My daughter has gone fuckin' cold. Losing my son hit her harder than she's letting on," he says with a beat down tone.

"ZZ, brother, I gotta get outta here for a while. Danick called. He has a shit ton of leads on his wife's murder." I hate that I am bringing this up, but he needs to know I won't be here. My friend needs my help, and I can't go back on my word.

"Your mentor, Danick?" ZZ rubs his nose between his fingers.

I give a jerk of my head to answer his question.

"And you gave him your word?"

"I did." I pull out my smokes, light one, and offer him one, too.

No brother goes back on their word.

"Shit, man, I've got to go to my son's parents, and she can't be left here without one of us. Storm refuses to let me do this on my own. Tatiana'll need you."

I already know that she does. I don't know what to do. I take a puff of my cig and inhale the biggest hit of nicotine.

"Take her with you."

He's got to be joking. I'm heading straight into shit worse than this, and he wants me to take her with me? He's fucking lost his ever loving mind!

"I'm dealin with the Italian mob, brother. It's safe here, and she won't be safe with me if she goes."

She can't go. She's fucked up enough over her brother dying, and now shooting this fucker. She thinks she isn't showing it, but she is. The pain laced in her words and her movement assures us of that.

"She can't," I argue.

ZZ takes a hit off of the cigarette and blows out some smoke. "Take her. Keep her safe, but let her see how dangerous shit actually is out there. It's easy here, but she thinks it isn't. This is not even one percent of the fucked up shit in this world."

He's right, but why the hell does he want me to take her with me and show her that? I do *not* understand his logic on this one.

"She shot a fucker! Take her with you, and see if she's really hardened or if it's a show. Do you think I would insist that my daughter go with you after losing my son? I trust you with her life. She'll see that this is peaches and cream compared to the shit you're about to get into. If you have problems and you have to send her back, I'll come get her if it gets serious."

There is no detouring him on this. He's deadset and not changing his mind. I don't have to take her, but he definitely has guilted me into it. I don't want her by herself, and if Storm and ZZ are going to Mace Jr.'s adoptive parents without her, I'm not leaving her here with the stress of Winter's pregnancy and all the other bullshit. I'll figure a way to sway her away from all the bad shit.

"I trust you with my daughter's life, Shadow. You wanted to be with her, so be with her," he says in a tired voice.

I do want to be with her, but at what cost? Her accidentally getting caught in the crossfire? Is my wanting to be with her worth that? I'll have to watch her back, my own, and help Danick at the same time, but it sounds like ZZ needs me to do this as bad as Danick needs my help.

ZZ is tired. Everyone is over it all. The bloodshed, the wars over drugs, business takeovers, and top that off with Winter's stressful pregnancy and Mace Jr.'s death. The entire club is depressed and morale is down a significant amount.

"I'll take her with me. We'll leave first thing in the morning, so you need to go tell her bye."

ZZ doesn't wait for me to say anything else. He takes off inside without another word. I've never prayed a day in my life, but I think I'm going to start. I don't think our club can handle any more loss.

***

Tatiana

Last night, when my dad told me that I was leaving with Shadow, I don't know what was going through my head. Dad warned me that I was heading towards shit I've never been around my entire life. The Italian mob. They're ruthless, cunning, and devious, he said.

For my own father to let me leave with Shadow is not something I would have expected after losing my brother, but knowing my father, this is to show me that my life is easier than others. He always has a plan behind his motives, and I am not naïve enough to think there isn't a motive behind this.

Mine and Shadow's relationship is brand new, and we're heading straight into more shit? Nothing like starting something and putting it to the test quite like this way. It'll definitely test our connection.

When Shadow said that we were heading to New Orleans, I was excited until his eyes turned cold on me. He laid it out to me after my dad left my room.

"This isn't a joke. You think Jamaica is heavy with crime! It ain't shit compared to going up against the American Mafia, aka the Italian Mafia. I'm still pissed ZZ wants me to take you with me. The only fuckin' reason you are goin with me is because I ain't about to leave you here by yourself, and to show you that your cold, callused new you is a bunch of bullshit."

It hurt, not going to lie, but he spoke part of the truth. If my own father thinks this is what it will take to show me the harsh world, so be it. I'm done arguing. I don't necessarily want this to be how Shadow and I start whatever it is that we're starting, but nothing is ever ordinary in our world.

So here it is the next morning, and I'm saying goodbye to our family to take a life lesson trip. That is what I've called it since last night. It seems suitable for this situation.

"Listen to his every word, baby girl," my dad whispers into my ear as he hugs me goodbye. "I love you, kiddo."

I squeeze him back and say that I love him, too.

When our goodbyes are over, my dad opens my car door, helps me get in, and shuts it behind me. Shadow climbs in and tells me to buckle up as he starts the Rover and we drive off towards New Orleans.

***

Acknowledgements

My husband – I couldn't have made it through this past year without you. I love you, bighead.

To my Mini Mes – You won't read this for another fifteen years, but know this, you two are the most amazing children a mom could have asked for. I love you, doodles!

Southern Mama - Kathryn Crane – We've come a long way since Talania. You are a main ingredient to my writing recipe. You push and teach me with each novel, and my only hope is that it never changes. I continue to grow because of you. I love you!

Julie Deaton – You're always there for me when I need you. I love you! (Readers, pay attention to Tatiana's middle name, coming in Schooling Me. Julie came up with it. ☺

And lastly, **Readers, Reviewers, Followers, Pimpers, My Breakneck Bitches, and Bloggers: A HUGE MASSIVE GIGANTIC THANK YOU!**

Contacting Crystal Spears

http://www.crystaldspears.com/

https://twitter.com/CrystalDSpears

http://www.pinterest.com/crystaldspears/

http://instagram.com/crystaldspears

https://www.goodreads.com/author/show/6451625.Crystal_Spears

Author.CrystalD.Spears@gmail.com

☆★☆★Series Order ☆★☆★

Seize Me - http://www.amazon.com/dp/B00DVAWGJ4

Withstanding Me - http://www.amazon.com/dp/B00EYE9A2W

Resenting Me - http://www.amazon.com/dp/B00MX1PZFO

Shadowing Me - http://www.amazon.com/dp/B00EYE9A2W

Discovering Me - http://www.amazon.com/dp/B00MWGZOC4

The Breakneck Series has lots of books, novellas, and novella shorts coming up as well.

Join my mailing list on my Contacting Crystal Spears Page to get all the lastest news!

***

27322752R00122

Made in the USA
Lexington, KY
28 December 2018